ROCK MEMOIR

ROCK MEMOIR

❧

BOOK 1 OF
THE BIRTH-FATHERS' CLUB
SERIES

Michele Kriegman

Reunion Land Press

ACKNOWLEDGEMENTS

I am fortunate to have met fathers in the foster care, adoption, and assisted reproduction technology worlds who inspired me with their integrity toward, and in some cases advocacy on behalf of, adopted-out and donor-conceived people. It is never too late for redemption, forgiveness, and gratitude, I believe.

My appreciation to the late Lynn C. Franklin of Lynn C. Franklin Associates, Ltd., International Literary Agency, who read an early version of The Birth-Fathers' Club in its entirety, offering guidance that has shaped the series for the better, and to my other beta reader, Mark A. Furman, for being my alpha and omega in wondrous ways.

Photo credits: author photo thanks to Mark Furman, and for the C. A. Feissner live photos, thanks to Sato Dai & the rest of the band.

CONTENTS

1

∽

Maybe you better sit down for this

Tony Silvio sat in his man cave strumming distractedly on an unplugged electric guitar. Once, many years ago, he was wandering around a house party in LA when he happened upon Jerry Garcia sitting quietly in the den, surrounded by a small crowd. They were discussing something in earnest—he could not remember what—but what struck him was Garcia sitting there like a bearded Buddha picking away very quietly on an Ovation acoustic guitar as naturally as breathing. Later over a shared joint Garcia told him that he played at least three hours a day—while eating breakfast, watching movies, whenever—so he could keep his fingers loose. It made sense to Tony, and he was young enough to want to try to change and become a better player. It was one of his few good habits and he picked it up early.

His man cave was not like most. There were no framed photos of favorite ballplayers, autographed sports shirts, or team-branded beer mugs. Even as a kid Tony had never been much interested in sports, and even less interested in jocks, preferring to listen to rock'n'roll and hang with his buddies in the park smoking dope and whistling at girls.

Alongside three platinum records in black frames and dozens of album covers, Tony's walls held two framed guitars—one signed by all the members of his first band, the other destroyed by Hendrix in 1967 at Monterey that Tony had bought at an auction a few years back. Set him back about $150,000, as he recalled. Funny story about that one—few realized that Hendrix had switched out his favorite guitar, a Stratocaster, for a much cheaper one before he smashed it and lit it on fire up on the stage. Tony really liked the fact that even a way-out stoned dude like Hendrix had enough common sense at the last second to not destroy his best axe. Unfortunately, Hendrix did not have the clarity—or the will—to save himself before the final OD. Tony, through the grace of his Higher Power and, to be honest, through dumb luck had stopped just before a similar end and pulled himself back up—with a lot of help.

His fingers idly brushed the striated metal strings, strumming a few chords, picking a few notes, not really heading anywhere but seeing if something might come up.

He was interrupted by the buzzing of his internal phone line. Bishop, his manager, aide-de-camp, and all-around organizer, was calling. Tony had nicknamed Bishop, "The Glove" because over the last seven years he became the outside layer that protected Tony Silvio from the daily vicissitudes of life as a rock star. Bishop the Glove fielded all calls, paid all bills, arranged all hotel rooms and travel schedules, freeing Tony up to focus on his core business—being the Tony Silvio Project.

More important, Bishop kept Tony straight in more ways than just organizing his life.

Tony picked up the phone.

"Sorry to bother you, but I have someone on the line that I think you should talk to."

"Who is it?"

"Um, Tony, I think it's just best if you talk to her and then you and I can talk about it."

It was not like Bishop to be so evasive, and Tony felt his old temper rising in his blood. What was with this secrecy all of a sudden? And he was suspicious that it was a "her" on the line—there were too many "hers" in his touring days to not immediately be on alert when he heard this. But then Tony thought that Bishop usually had a damned good reason for what he did, so he bit back a harsh retort and said, "Okay, I guess the Gloves just came off."

Bishop chuckled at the reference and must have patched it through because the second line on the phone began blinking.

Instead of picking it up right away, Tony stared at it for a few seconds, then paced over to the window and back. When faced with a tricky situation, Tony Silvio was a master at finding a way to avoid the thing completely. It used to be the key part of being the Tony Silvio Project. It still was his first impulse, but he had learned to let it pass so he could listen to his better self. It told him to take this call.

He took a deep breath and punched the second line. "Hi, it's Tony Silvio."

"Hi," said the female voice on the other end.

"Who is this?"

"My name's Jessica. Maybe you better sit down for this."

Tony actually did what she suggested.

"Do you remember a party in Boise in 1989?"

"Sugar, I don't remember the 80s."

He habitually fell into his funny-guy routine, trying to deflect where this might be going, push it into the fantasy realm of The Tony Silvio Project.

"Oh, you've got a sense of humor," she sounded pleased, "We haven't met yet, but we have a connection who you might remember."

Certainly he had not derailed her. He felt like this was turning into some kind of interview. "What's this about?"

"Uh, maybe this should ring a bell. I was born in November 1989," she said then paused.

"Like I said—"

"Yeah, you 'don't remember the 80s.' You really are the way my birth-mom described!"

A little shift, he could almost know what was coming if he could only clear his head. Before he could, she burst out, "You're my father. My *birth-father*. I'm your daughter."

Damn.

It sounded like she whimpered; he must have said it out loud. He didn't mean that.

"No, I didn't mean it in a bad way. I meant it like 'damn, uh, that's really great', I'm surprised is all," and he hoped she believed him. His heartbeat *was* picking up its tempo with excitement. But his body also thrummed with that old impulse to run, hide, escape from being pinned down by this intense thing that suddenly was blossoming over the phone while he sat in his previously safe room.

He heard her talking, but part of his mind was racing in a thousand directions at once, trying to figure out a clever way to get out of this trap, to push the problem on someone else. A small voice in the back of his head was yearning for the blissful fog of being drunk or stoned; that would buy him some time here. Once a junkie, always a junkie.

But he also heard the voice of his old Narcotics Anonymous sponsor, "So, how's that running away working for ya'?" And so Tony keyed back in to Jessica's voice over the phone.

"My birth-mother said she told you but, like, you didn't react. She wasn't sure it registered. She said she wasn't even a girlfriend. No one bothered to even ask you to sign a TPR or anything."

"TPR?"

"Termination of Parental Rights. It's a form birth-fathers are supposed to sign when they give up their kid." *There was that term again, "birth-father". He turned it over in his mind, feeling its texture a bit.* "You were so wasted and busy on tour that you couldn't have fought for custody or stopped the adoption even if you *cared*." She said it matter-of-factly as if she had been there.

What was he supposed to say to this? 'Even if you cared'.

"If I knew, I would have cared," he answered, not knowing if he was sidestepping it or jumping right in, "Just 'cause she said she told me doesn't mean she did." Then he added a little lamely, "Who—who was she?"

He heard a sigh on the other end.

Instead of pressing for an answer he filled the silence himself, playing Tony Silvio again. "I've loved a lot of ladies, you know."

He kept going like a seasoned gambler who keeps up the monologue as he deals a new hand, "I was in love with every one of them. Hey, you never told me her name. I guess you'd want to meet me. Why don't you come down? You play anything? If you do maybe you can sit in."

He must have been in his fifties but she thought the way he revved up and drawled out his speech made him sound like a slacker nineteen-year-old. She answered him, "Cyrena Banks was her name. You and your band did a concert there, in Boise, and there was an after party up at some lodge."

He rapidly searched his memory, sifting through so many parties after concerts, so many groupies in big cities and little towns, each wanting a piece of his glory and him willing to give it up for a night, carefree with no strings attached. Pure pleasure, reveling in a gluttony that few would ever experience. Boise, a lodge in the mountains, snow......

"Damn, you mean that crazy bearskin rug chick? Man, I remember it now, it was so cold I thought my—"

She quickly shut him down. "Uh, I don't really want to hear about that part. I guess I'm mostly interested in family history, medical, that kind of stuff."

Tony's mind was still tripping back to that night, suddenly coming out of the mists of his past, clearer now. They had played a gig in a smallish venue called The Zoo in Boise, a large club for that town but much smaller than what they usually played. A favor from their then-manager to The Zoo's owner, as he recalled. No one in the band was happy to have to drive in their custom bus over the mountains from Portland, a real city, to this tiny bandbox of a town south of Walla Walla, for Christ's sake. But their manager insisted. What they found was a crazy dedicated music scene made up of college dudes and off-the-grid hippies plus a bunch of super rich kids whose families had chateaus up in Sun Valley, slumming down in Boise for the night. The coke was unbelievable, pure blue flake as deep as the snow outside the hall. That he remembered fondly.

Somehow, they all wound up in one of those chateaus much much later that night, champagne and coke in equal measure, and at one point he found himself talking to an unbelievably beautiful raven-haired chick wearing a white fox coat, white leather pants, and knee-hugging leather boots. Frankly, he had seen a hundred girls like her, there had to be at least three or four at every single party; he thought perhaps they were all related or cloned or something.

But this one had a special twinkle, actually more like a dare, in her chocolate brown eyes, and when she leaned forward to kiss him he fell into it with abandon. She molded herself to him even before he'd had the chance to use his signature move, his palm pressed low against the small of a girl's back, tilting her pelvis into his. She was warm, smelling of vodka soaked watermelon but the way she smiled up at him with her perfect torso, climbing him like a pole, made him think of the snow coursing through her veins as well.

Out of the corner of his eye he thought he might have seen Maria watching from across the room, her long hair swept up in a chignon. He couldn't be sure. Yes, Maria was already in his life back then but he hadn't thought about settling down with her yet. Then he was hearing this other babe whisper in his ear, "Have you ever made it on a bearskin rug in the snow?"

2

Sowing

He forgot Maria. The idea of the rug intrigued him; he could almost feel its soft fur on his back as she sat astride him. But in the snow? He was not so sure about that one. Despite all the coke, he was a bit nervous as she smilingly pulled him to the back door of the chateau and out onto the snow-covered deck.

There was a blast of horizon with the distant dark vision of the nighttime Rockies filling half the sky above Boise. His lungs froze slightly with his first breath. He suddenly realized it was cold out and maybe she was a friggin' freak. A billion sharp stars sparkled in the cold night air.

"Uh, look, it's kinda, you know, cold out here, darlin'?"

She just laughed and pulled him by his shirtfront down the stairs to the snow-covered lawn below. Tony started to get a little worried about being alone with her, isolated, in the snow, under the stars. But she kept walking through the snow and came to a small house—more like a hut—that he hadn't noticed before. Opening the door, he saw that there was a potbellied stove inside, and on the floor the biggest damned polar bear rug he had ever imagined. Now THIS was going to be okay, he thought, as she turned into him and they fell as one into the room. He did not often remember the ladies he laid on tour, but this one, well, there was something different about her, something memorable even for him.

He broke the reverie and asked into the phone, "Where are you anyway?"

Jessica answered, "I'm an hour and a half outside New York, halfway to Philly."

He did not know what to do next, what was expected of him. She seemed to know a lot of details that only that girl—her birth-mother!—might know, but then, again, maybe someone else at that party had seen them go out, or heard the story? A part of his mind was scrambling to think of how to figure out if she was really his daughter or if this was some sort of a touch to get close to his money, not that he had all that much left these days, but no one knew that except for Bishop the Glove, his wife Maria, and his creditors.

Maybe he should demand a genetic test or something? Yet deep inside he knew that she was not gaming him, that this was real. It just felt right, and he decided with some wonder and more than a little of the old Tony Silvio brio to go with that for now.

"Um, I guess...I guess we should, you know, meet some-time?" he sputtered, still hoping she would say no, and he could just send some autographed photos.

"Yah, sure, that would be nice."

"Hey, I have a book signing out there in a month, near Philly. Not exactly the best place. Or we could meet in the Big

Apple before then. Just one-on-one, maybe catch a cuppa?" Tony slipped into his pseudo-British invasion cockney.

She agreed immediately.

That simple.

Tony was stunned, it was happening all too fast for him; clearly, she had thought this all through before she called him. He hated this feeling, like she was a step ahead of him. Usually he used crazy humor and rapid shifts in mood and topic to stay in control, keeping everyone off balance, dancing to his tune, wondering what would come next. Yet he sensed that this would be the absolutely wrong time and place for that.

Instead they began working out the details of a coffee shop breakfast. Just when he felt things were back on a safe track, she suddenly asked, "Do I have any brothers or sisters?"

Damn. This time he kept that to himself, and said, "No, me and my old lady never had kids. I was her kid. Well, she might have wanted kids. We always planned on it but the timing was never right."

"TMI."

"What, you like acronyms a lot? Hell: TPR, TMI. Listen, sugar, I at least owe you a meeting, if you want one."

* * *

That's how classic rocker Tony Silvio found out. He wasn't touring much anymore although when he did he could fill medium sized venues. His memoir, *Birth of the True*, was in galleys when he got the call. His editor wanted the story of his birth-daughter added in. The whole story. The existence of a daughter would make good copy.

Tony refused. There was enough sex, drugs and rock'n'roll

that he didn't need to cop on his own kid's conception. No, he made sure it didn't make it into print. Like Tony told Jessica, his new daughter with Cyrena Banks, it wouldn't have been appropriate.

But the real reason was Maria. She was the smartest, most sensual woman he'd ever known. And Maria had agreed to marry him twenty years ago. She'd stood by him before, during and after the wild days and through his many attempts at recovery. She didn't need to read in print the details of his dalliance.

3

The Wild Oat

It had been a few years since Tony wrote a new tune, or at least one he was ready to take into the studio to record. But he was starting to feel the itch again, yearning for the creative moment to hit. Now that he was clear and clean, free from the soul-sapping dance of debt and spending and drinking and cheating and drugging, he wondered if that old sense would come back.

When he wrote his best songs, the ones that became rock anthems that you heard on classic rock stations and in ballparks to this day, they almost sprang from him fully formed, by-passing his mind and coming straight from somewhere inside him. Truth be told, he was scared, petrified, that he had lost that. Maybe it was all the drugs that burned it out of him; but he was even more frightened that perhaps he could only do it because of the drugs and the booze and the crazy living. No way was he going back to that insanity again. And yet, the thought of never feeling that moment of grace when the song is perfect and you just know it in your bones...

Part of him was curious to meet this daughter, see how much she looked like him. But another instinct was to try to make this all go away as fast as possible. The two impulses were warring inside his head and he almost missed her answering "yes" that day.

After Tony hung up the phone he stared blankly out the floor-to-ceiling window that looked over forty acres of woods, his pride and joy. He called it his "prayer window", the one place where he could sometimes really feel his Higher Power, as they called it in AA's Big Book. His mind was furiously trying to process all the possible ways that this new reality could play out. Should he tell his wife Maria? No, how could he? Imagine her reaction when she found out he had a kid out there after all these years of him putting her off on that one! But how would he keep her from finding out? Well, he would push that one out until after he had that breakfast with Jessica.

Somewhere in the back of his mind Tony knew that lying to Maria about his daughter was falling back into his old addictive thinking pattern of behavior. What was it that they said at meetings? "The truth shall set you free." But Tony just did not have the courage, or the recovery strength apparently, to face into the look that he knew Maria would give him. No, even with the guilt he was feeling, that would have to wait until he had done more processing himself.

"Jessica," he said out loud, amazed that he had a daughter out there. He watched a doe and her fawn stepping through the trees near the edge of his lawn while he rolled that thought around his brain. The Serenity Prayer bounced through his mind. *God, grant me the serenity to accept the things I cannot change.* Time to turn it over and let Higher Power run with it, as they said at meetings. He took a few deep breaths to try to find some serenity, and then the thought came to him in a flash. He needed to call his sponsor, and fast.

In the end, the one-on-one meeting with Jessica never happened. Tony's schedule was simply too booked solid what with the promos for the book release and the practices for the related concert tour. The first sets of rehearsals for the tour were really rough, and the instinct that had guided him to the top and kept him there for decades told Tony that he and his musicians needed more time to run through the sets, and with as little distraction as possible. So Bishop read between the lines, pivoted quickly, and invited Jessica to the studio instead. This had the added benefit that it would be on comfortable terrain for Tony and fun for her. And since the sessions were closed, there would be no prying paparazzi.

Tony was with the rest of the band lounging in the studio while the producer was in the sound booth laying in a guitar track, when Jessica walked in, accompanied by Bishop.

Tony had spent some sleepless nights wondering what she would look like, and more importantly, what he would say when he first met his own daughter. It was not something that most people had to confront in their lives. There were no self-help books or websites on how-to-meet-your-grown-progeny for the first time.

He tried to recall news shots of soldiers returning home from a long tour in Afghanistan and holding their babies for the first time, the look on the soldiers' faces a mix of pride, awe, wonder, and more than a little bit of discomfort. Did they have an innate ability to recognize their own offspring? Or were they a bit stunned that the kid looked like any other kid to them, when they were expecting something magical and immediate?

But those were babies. Tony was about to meet an adult, a grown young woman who had a personality and twenty years of life experiences; a mind of her own. Babies will accept you so long as you treat them with love and kindness. How would his adult daughter react to seeing him for the first time? Would she be repelled by his very public history of craziness that was as much a part of the Tony Silvio brand as his music? Would she be willing to meet him once but then dismiss him as so much noise and smoke?

It surprised Tony to realize he was certain that if she rejected him it would hurt even more than knowing he had missed watching her grow up. Both Bishop and his sponsor had warned him that it was possible, and he had cavalierly blown them off with one of his typical funny jokes—"No girl can resist Tony Silvio!"—but as he watched her come through the solid metal door to the studio, he suddenly felt desperate to make sure that she would accept him, like him, and want to see him again. The only other person he felt like this about was Maria, he realized. And with that thought another wave of guilt washed over him, knowing that he had hidden this meeting from Maria. It lent a somewhat sour note to meeting Jessica.

He turned to playing a few measures of rhythm and flashed what he hoped was a welcoming smile to his daughter but missed a chord in the process. He raised his hand in a "just a minute" signal, and returned to working out the backing for the current song.

Their producer asked, "Hey, Tony, you wanna take a break?"

Tony signaled "no" and focused. He put the tingle of energy that was beginning to soar up his spine into his playing. Nailed it.

"That's a gooder," he heard from the producer behind the mixing board. "That's a wrap, everyone take five."

Tony looked up and put the guitar down. He burst out laughing. The joy of the music. The fact of this kid, his kid, standing in the studio while he cut a new track. It all felt right, balanced, like it was meant to be. Tony did a quick internal check and, yes, he was certain that he was not deluding himself, not looking to manipulate the moment. Now he was ready to greet her and bounced off his chair.

"Hey, Jessica!" he called but noticed that she was standing there with some hesitation in her posture. Of course, she must be wondering what to do, how to be, he reasoned, so he slowed his heartbeat down and approached her a little more slowly.

Tony and Jessica stood face to face for the first time, quietly looking into each other's eyes, trying to decide if there was something familiar there. For Tony it was one of those proverbial moments when time stands still and everything around you—people, the room, the sounds—disappears as if behind the closed door of a sound booth when you cut a solo.

Tony held out his hand to Jessica. Nodding slightly, as if she had confirmed something for herself, she sidestepped his arm and gave him a big hug, her head held back a bit so she could still see his face.

The move surprised Tony, and for a minute he was frozen. A warmth ran through him and he wrapped his arms around Jessica, pulling her close to his heart. And again, time stood still for a little while. When she slid out of his grasp and took a step back she was both giggling and crying. He laughed again as he wiped a tear from her pretty eyes.

"Look at you! Looklooklooklooklook. This is my baby girl." Tony was feeling the way he wanted to feel, on top of the world, and there wasn't a line of cocaine in sight.

"Yup," she gulped and just beamed up at him.

Suddenly the rest of the world came back into focus as Tony realized that the entire studio—band members and technical crew—were watching them in silent astonishment, wondering what was going on with Tony now. Tony wrapped one arm around Jessica's shoulders and, standing side by side, he announced to them all that "This here is my little girl! It's the first time we have ever met, so I didn't have time to buy those pink chocolate cigars to hand out!"

After a stunned moment of silence, a chorus broke out.

"Wow, man, that is so cool!"

"Congrats Tony, rad story, man!"

One of the guitarists started playing Paul Simon's *"Mother and Child Reunion"* to guffaws of laughter.

Jessica put her bag down on one of the chairs and then came back to stand next to Tony as someone snapped some pictures on a cell phone. Tony hoped that they would not wind up on People Magazine's website, at least not before he had a chance to discuss Jessica with Maria.

They looked at each other some more. Jessica was gasping

and breathy and he had no clue what he was saying. They told him later it was a string of cusses, happy ones.

The whole entourage moved out to the hall and across to a meeting room where Bishop had ordered in platters and salads. Gone were the old studio days of liquid lunches washing down burritos and fried chicken. Their new fare was more Mediterranean diet inflected with Perrier water chasers, food befitting men worried about heart attacks and widening spare tires—one of Tony's favorite lines was that his sixpack had become a keg.

Jessica quickly proved to be a girl who loved to tell a good story. And so with little coaxing from the band members, she told theirs: how she had spit into a vial and sent her sample off to Ancestrology on a whim one day, only to be shocked with a complete paternal DNA match for, of all people, Tony Silvio!

Then she reenacted the phone call, throwing her head back and doing a dead-on imitation of how Tony sounded, shocked and cocky all once, "'Babe, I can't even remember the '80's!'"

The band broke out in knowing laughs, casting wry glances at Tony while he scowled good naturedly back at them, enjoying being the center of attention again.

She could hold a room, just like him, Tony thought with pride. When she spoke, her voice carried a warm, rich, musical vibration and suddenly one of the guys asked if she could sing. Her eyes slid over to him and he nodded. Didn't Warren Zevon or Van Morrison cut tracks with their kids? The thought sent a thrill down his spine as he pictured standing on a stage with Jess singing harmony next to him and the crowds adoring them both.

Jess, he was calling her Jess in his mind already, until suddenly Tony felt like he was having an out-of-body experience, not in a bad way, perhaps, but it felt like it was all moving too fast. He was not sure how he was supposed to be reacting. Just a few weeks ago he had no idea she existed, and suddenly here she was, in his life, in his studio, in his picture of the future, for God's sake. He had never in his life envisioned himself as having a kid, someone that he created, who shared his genes, his essence. It sent him hurtling into a whole different conception of who he was.

Hell, he hadn't even been looking. But this was good. This felt easy and comfortable and real. Tony leaned forward in his chair, his hands resting on his knees; someone was talking, but he announced, "You know what, this feels good, real good. I can't believe we haven't met before...Jess. Feels like I've always known you."

Someone chimed in, "She sure looks like you Ton'."

"Remember when your cousins came up? She's got the same coloring as all of you.."

Tony laughed, "Yes, we do. She looks just like my tomato cousins from Macon, Georgia. Southern fried tomatoes."

The room laughed. But, as often was the case, Tony was using humor to deflect attention from his real emotions. Because deep inside he actually did feel an immediate, strong, almost primordial connection with this young woman sitting in his sound studio. It was confusing enough to make him suspicious of the sensation—was his mind playing tricks on him, knowing that they shared 50% of their genes? Yet, the feeling was persistent, powerful, and he wondered if this is how all fathers felt when they watched their grown-up children.

Tony surveyed Jessica some more. She pulled out a scrapbook decorated with all sorts of colors and art paper. She was pretty creative, he could see. Now she was sitting on the chair, had every man's eyes when she held up the scrapbook to walk them through it. Baby pictures. Birthday parties and blowing out candles. Family picnics by a lake with much shorter parents. Low-cut prom dress and a date that looked like he really dug her. Cap and gown. A thousand beach pictures.

Before heading to the studio this morning Tony actually grabbed one old baby picture, another taken by his parents with his high school band, and a family picnic under cherry trees, and stuck all three in an envelope. He handed it now to Jessica.

She looked at the baby picture and teared up, "Awwww, you were so cute."

He heard some of the guys echo, "Awww, so cuuuuuu-uute."

Jessica spread the photos out on the table and reached down for her phone, explaining, "I wanna take these."

Did he imagine it, or was she also looking at these photos with the same genetic recognition he was feeling?

"Keep 'em," Tony himself was choking up. She stared at him with pure love. It hit him that, "she loves me and she just met me and she doesn't want anything out of me."

He tried to think of something to say about each of the photos. Everyone laughed some more. When after a while Tony paused and tilted back in his chair, it was the cue for some of the others to start sharing stories. Tony was surprised that anyone else had stories of lost relatives and family secrets.

"I had an uncle. I didn't meet him, hell, until I was grown either. He was a gambler, you see..."

"Brian's ex-girlfriend. Remember we met him playing in Rocky's Cellar?"

Tony nodded.

"Now she might or might not have been pregnant, never heard for sure. The way they were talking and then she just drops off the tour? I've always wondered...."

"We had neighbors upstairs that adopted from Nepal. They brought home a little girl, and they had all these silver bangles and anklets for her. Cute but didn't speak English yet. Then they moved to the 'burbs...."

Jessica sat rapt through it all. Stealing glances at him, he was aware, like a kid with a crush. He realized that she had probably fantasized about her missing father, had heard her birthmom tell stories about him and already knew his career from the tabloids and the Internet.

Tony had a small worry that he would not be able to live up to such hype, such fantasies. He could hear his sponsor reminding him to take it all one day at a time, trust in his Higher Power, and see where it all led rather than trying to force it to conform to his own ideas of where it should go.

Finally, the car Bishop had scheduled showed up and it was time to end. Tony scratched the back of his neck as he stood up and stretched.

"So, hey, this was great, really great, and we need to meet up again, real soon, okay?" he said to Jessica.

She nodded, and then he quickly wrapped her in a huge bear hug, feeling her arms wrap around him and pull him tight as well. He almost lost it then, but he pulled back and they smiled at each other warmly, again as if they had known each other forever, shared a special bond, just the two of them.

After the door closed behind her, Tony stood silently, thinking that this was perhaps one of the best days of his life. He suddenly felt connected to the future in a way that had not existed for him just a few hours before. He had a daughter out there, a young woman who was just starting out on her own journey through life, who would carry on his legacy in ways he could not even imagine. It was heady, intoxicating in a good way.

And then he thought, "Maria."

How was he going to share this with Maria, whom he had not even told yet about Jessica? Suddenly the euphoria of meeting his daughter was freighted with the guilt and shame of falling back into his old pattern of hiding inconvenient truths from his wife. Just like the drinking and drugging and women and money shenanigans. It sat like a wet mass in the pit of his stomach.

Well, he realized, it was time to do the 12 Step "work" he practiced as part of his recovery. For this one, it meant seeing how his holding back may have harmed Maria and then figuring out how best to make amends to her. This simple "work" always made the burden of his thoughts or feelings lighter. He needed that real bad.

Returning to the sound booth, he picked up his guitar while the others were reassembling from lunch, and launched into a mournful solo rendition of the Stone's *"You Can't Always Get What You Want"*.

The producer was smart enough to catch it on tape, suspecting that it would one day become a great bootleg release on a Tony Silvio compilation.

4

Why didn't you ever tell me?

Tony was almost bouncing on his toes after meeting with Jessica. It gave him the courage he needed to come clean with Maria.

When he got in the house, she called out to him and he found her in one of the extra practice rooms—she liked their acoustics—where holding a wide paintbrush in her hand she looked up from a project. The brush was drenched in deep blue glittering paint and she stood next to a rocking chair. She smiled that beautiful smile and said, "I'm painting this with stripes. Midnight cobalt and sunset pink, you like?"

"I like."

She was happy. This was a moment he wanted to stretch out. He flashed on a walk they took together last Sunday at Duke Farms, a large private nature preserve that had been opened to the public by the estate of the tobacco heiress, Doris Duke. There among the profusion of wild flowers and families walking on the gentle paths, one of those crazy Tony Silvio Project things happened that always gave him a thrill. Suddenly somewhere from the other side of a field of mauve grasses, a smartphone rang out, "*Shoot the Alarm*", his biggest hit. Tony grinned at Maria by his side.

She smiled back up at him and then he just kept smiling and smiling to himself. He stepped into the studio and sat on the floor, "Maria, there's something I need to tell you."

Maria turned her back to him, ostensibly to put the brush back in the paint can, but the move was also intended to give her a moment to compose herself.

There had been far too many such admissions over the years, Maria thought. They always started out the same way, and they never ended well for her. She straightened up and turned back around wearing her best game face. She was still and waiting.

***

He decided to just say it straight up. He promised himself he would be kind but honest. What was it his friend in the 12 Step program used to say? Say what you mean, mean what you say, but don't say it mean. That was it. But even still he wavered as he wondered if this confession would mean they'd never have an afternoon like last Sunday again.

They'd been through this before every time he decided to come clean and go into rehab or into a new program. There were also a few affairs that she blew out of proportion. He'd be patient until he couldn't stand it anymore. The kicker was the paternity suit which, mind you, got dismissed after he agreed to take a DNA test. So he knew the drill. Maria did too. This time there would be no DNA test to bail him out, no slippery evasions or half-truths to try to gaslight her once again.

Maria said nothing. She just listened to his confession with a slightly distracted air, as if she were in the room with him physically but mentally and spiritually she was at a distant and safe remove.

Maria asked a question or two and it seemed okay for now.

But he knew with certainty that a day later or an hour later, just like always, she'd ask more questions each with a stinging edge. Or he'd be affectionate and all he'd get was a turned shoulder or a terse retort.

He told Maria how he had shared it with his sponsor, and how he had managed to keep this mess out of the book. It was sort of a shame, now that he'd met Jessica. He said that he wasn't bringing this out in the book, even though it was great timing and even though the publicity crew wanted to play up Jessica.

"They KNOW?" she finally blurted out, exasperated and embarrassed.

He sighed, "Yes."

"You told them?!"

"Yes. No. I don't know. They found out."

"'They found out,'" Maria whispered back bitterly. "Right, once again everyone knows except for me. They're going to use it. That girl will probably sell the story herself."

"No, she's not like that. I love you, Maria," Tony said, his voice full of despair and self-pity.

"Don't you even."

In utter frustration he closed with, "What did you expect,

what did you really expect back when you were dating a rock'n'roller who lived most of the year on the road?"

She gave him a look of sheer disgust, turned her back on him, and left him standing alone in the room trying to figure out why he had once again hurt the one person he truly loved. Maybe the real point was that he could not love anyone but himself, he wondered at some deep level of his mind.

Tony's agent came up with a compromise: Jessica and Cyrena stayed out of the memoir. Instead, he'd save the story for the book tour and podcast circuit where it took off like wildfire. Stories quickly circulated on the fan pages about his meeting with Jessica at the recording session, including photos of the attractive young woman grinning next to her new-found father.

At some readings Tony spiced it up for the press with a few details that could have been true. More often it was easy enough to toss off the line that he didn't remember the party and it only built the legend. At book signings it would get laughter—knowing laughter or nervous laughter—he didn't know. But it sure made them want to buy the book.

On a typical interview with an entertainment reporter who caught up with Tony at home Tony said, "I told the girl, 'You're in charge of the pace of this reunion, honey.'" The one and only Tony Silvio was soaking several grain-fed buffalo steaks in ginger ale at the time, his Alcoholics Anonymous sponsor having urged him to switch out the beer. So ginger ale became the new brewskie and it was a signature prep ingredient at his eponymous Chelsea restaurant, Tony Silvio's.

"But, in the assured Silvio state of extremis, we have caught up with more meaningful father-daughter time in the past twelve months than a lot of fathers and daughters probably ever get." He paused. "I'm sure if Vick Sledge found his long-lost son it'd be fun. But not this much fun." Vick Sledge was a punk era memoir writer. He'd been through several calendars' worth of 28-day rehab check-ins and was rumored to have fathered a son.

* * *

Tony's rock diary *Birth of the True* covered just one side of the story, one side of life up to and after his slow climb to recovery. One recovery, then the next, only to uncover another addiction another compulsion. Each recovery promised new hope. Each delivered part of the promise. Each included a round of confessions and amends, as defined by him, the pop star, thought Maria.

Rock memoirs like this didn't recount what it meant for her—all the nights alone—the suspense. It was the wife, the girlfriend, the estranged children that nursed themselves on suspense masked as hope.

The rock star never really *got* that this suspense was soaked with fear, the blood tests for AIDS, the swabs for STDs. But Maria had read other men's rock'n'roll memoirs as Tony worked on his. As much as she loved their life, especially at the beginning, the memoirs themselves lack suspense. For the reader the thrill is voyeurism, like reading a high-end catalogue.

But it wasn't just music and the high times. Buried within these memoirs were the stories of other men who shared the

Tony Silvio Project's secret: hidden fatherhood. Famously, there was Mick Jagger, Keith Richards, and the late Brian Jones of the Rolling Stones (well, his girlfriend's memoir *Not Fade Away* anyway). The list went on: Rod Stewart, Roger Daltrey, Steven Tyler, Ted Nugent, and Tom Petty.

Rock memoir was a loose term, Maria decided, because it crossed music genres. There was Drake who wrote the rap, "*March 14th*" about coming to terms with being someone's father—but only after a rival rapper, Pusha T, called him out in "The Story of Adidon", rapping, *"You are hiding a child / Let that boy come home / Deadbeat motherf–ka, playin' border control."* Drake came clean with *"She not my lover like Billie Jean, but the kid is mine."*

There was David Crosby, of Stills, Crosby, Nash & Young, who was briefly an anonymous sperm donor before becoming an involved parent.

Hank Williams, Sr., whose daughter published a book on proving his paternity, he eventually recognized her. It took until country singer Tim McGraw was in his teens before baseball great Tug McGraw acknowledged him as his son. After that, Tug joked, *"It took me this long and now all anyone knows me as is Tim McGraw's father!"*

Then there was Screamin' Jay Hawkins. Hawkins surely held some kind of record. Over thirty-seven adults claimed him as their father while he actually claimed that he fathered over fifty kids on tour.

Readers didn't get to submerge themselves in a personal lake of suspense the way Maria did. She bathed in it. Knew it intimately. There was one month when someone kept calling, then just sniffled quietly as Maria repeated, "Hello, who is this?" before hanging up.

The next time it was Tony who took the call in another part of the house. All she heard on his end was, "...my house again!" before he slammed down the phone.

Then the calls only came two or three times more. Not even a breath before she'd hear a click and the line went dead.

Sometimes she got worn down: she stopped asking "why?" when he called over his shoulder that he would do his own laundry.

His first manager, smarmy, opportunistic. When all the details came out what had been going on, she looked back and wasn't sure if that shapeshifter made more money from their music or from dealing in the parking lot.

The suspense continued. After a while in AA Tony was going to a meeting a week. Started talking the talk, even admitted to some of her accusations. But, for her, the suspense continued. At first, she thought he had been saved. He started talking "godtalk". They even went to a prayer service after a few months, went almost every week for six, eight months. Yet, still Maria held her breath, doubting, knowing that despite the superficial appearance, deep down Tony was still Tony Silvio and that she could not trust that he had really, truly, fundamentally changed. And she feared that he might never be able to.

* * *

She remembered a backstage visit early on in their courtship. He was waiting for her and took her to the green room to avoid the mayhem where the groupies, roadies and other bandmembers were meeting in clutches. She would rather not imagine what was happening around her. Instead they joked about the fistful of irises and pussy willow she brought backstage with her, long brown and green rods with royal purple and yellow sprays alongside silvered nobs. They joked that it was a man-bouquet.

Later, on tour, she would remember a springtime tour stop when she was bused from Madison Square Stadium with the other wives and girlfriends to tour an iris garden in Montclair an hour west. Then the wives and girlfriends were bussed to dinner theater far from Broadway. The band and the roadies stayed behind. Someone had them all showered and tucked in, sound asleep, by the time the girls returned.

In Tokyo they were bused from Budokan to Meiji Shrine where iris fields were planted in flows like a stage set river. She didn't wonder what the boys in the band were doing those afternoons. An hour from an arena they played in Indiana—Indianapolis? Gary? Bloomington?—there was even an iris "lake" garden. Lonely, she wandered with the other wives and girlfriends remembering the innocence of that man-bouquet and trying not to wonder who Tony might be with this afternoon.

* * *

In the early days of Tony's recovery, a true believer who'd been clean eighteen years said something that lifted Maria's soul and tickled her mind: the 12 Steps program is America's gift to spirituality. Tony shared with her the 12 Steps he was "working" as they say in the lingo.

Now many years in, Maria knew what most people didn't know about 12 Steps. It was this: once your beautiful loser ran through AA and Narcotics Anonymous, even Sexaholics Anonymous, they arrived at the addict's and gambler's final stop: Debtors Anonymous. The bar tabs caught up with them, the grandiose lifestyle that he could not really afford suddenly came to a screaming halt under a mountain of debt.

Another thing she knew: those 12 Steps required that they make amends to those they harmed to the extent that they acknowledged the harm. On the flip side were the ones like herself whom she called "the *amended* ones".

"It caught up with us too," she thought. "All the nights we stayed home alone.

We were the one that the family drama-king took for granted, what they call the co-dependent. At best we were the objects of their stories they told to rapt and supportive audiences at countless meetings in church basements, sitting on cold metal folding chairs. If they made you live through enough drama and told their stories really well, your private humiliations could even be told by your humiliator at a *regional 12 Step conference*. You were grist and they, with heart-rending emotion of course, were the mill.

Tony the musician was becoming a new kind of rock star on the alcohol recovery speaker circuit. His celebrity had opened this door, yes, but it was his colorful delivery and willingness to expose their personal life that promised a whole new career. He would confess into the microphone the pain he had inflicted on her, the more detail the better, she supposed. The hushed audience relived his bad boy drinking days vicariously, a voyeurism of righteousness, and when he was done with his alcologue, they applauded.

Meanwhile she stayed home alone, read novels, and streamed movies. Quiet. Sometimes the greatest drama was the snow falling outside her window as she waited.

She was startled and then weary when it turned out his performances in these "rooms", as the 12-steppers referred to their meetings, turned out to be more of the same pre-rehab suspense. Just as when he was on tour, she was caught in a cycle of suspense and suspicion, unable to trust anything Tony told her. He'd come home an hour late from a meeting. If she pressed, he'd say it was talking to a newcomer. But under the guise of "AA Anonymity", Tony would not share with her who he was with or what they said, leaving her frozen out and distrustful.

He was just talking, he would say, "sharing strength, hope and recovery with someone in need", doing his Step 12 work by giving back—and there was perhaps a fifty-percent chance that it was true. Fifty-percent chance that anything he said was true. She lived in dread of the pendulum swinging from confession back to lies. It had happened twice in their marriage. Both times made her sick in the pit of her stomach.

This time, Maria thought, they might not make it through to the other side.

She had finally grown bored.

She was bored with his tangles of vagueness, and numbers or stories that just didn't add up. She was bored with all the missed dinners. She was bored with the no-longer even dreamed of trips that were promised but then forgotten in a haze of one addiction or another.

In fact, after so much patience and quiet suffering, so many loud arguments and nights going to sleep in anger and waking up just as mad, Maria had an epiphany. She was seriously considering leaving Tony Silvio. However, she thought to herself, she might want out but not without some drama of her own first.

She concluded that she had let herself become anaesthetized by the importance of being someone else's anchor, someone else's rock to come home to. Now that was wearing off. Anchors and rocks are inanimate. She was tired of being inanimate.

Would he be *her* rock now, would he be the one by her side if she tried to drive them off the rails? She was curious enough to pose the question. But it wasn't the reason for her plan.

Truth was, a guy who's been messing around with substances and other partners didn't have much left to offer. Sure, she'd flattered him, as much to ease her co-dependent celibacy as anything else. But there were more direct, more *satisfying* ways for her to unhook herself from a relationship with a sometime recovered sexaholic, weren't there?

5

~

Maria

Maria was out for justice now.

She had been attracted to Tony Silvio's music first, then his outsized frontman personality. Once she was with the band, she liked being near that lifestyle but not of it; one of the roadies even nicknamed her Mother Maria for her calm, no-drugs, moderate drinking approach to letting her hair down. Then once she and Tony Silvio settled down, if settling down is what you could call it, the wedding vows transformed her further. She felt something at the altar, but he was there because she wanted to marry in the Church and he sensed she would leave him if he didn't cross that divide.

Today, twenty years out, she was beginning to question the value of all this time being Santa Maria. She wanted to find the right thing to say to Tony so the scales would fall from his eyes and he'd realize how bad he'd been to her. How self-centered he was. Once, a well-meaning addiction counselor told her that his using was a kind of obsessive-compulsive disorder—OCD they called it—and brain scans showed it was related to anxiety which was related to depression. For some the funky brain structure could even flag a mood disorder like manic-depression and all the snowstorms of coke and el niños of alcohol simply meant her poor Tony Silvio was self-medicating. The counselor hinted to Maria that Tony might have underlying depression like Van Morrison. She still remembered when Tony went up and sang a duet with Van after he spotted them in the audience in Dublin. She had gasped not only at how beautiful the two sounded together, but that Van dedicated the ballad to her.

Sitting in the upstairs' bedroom swing, Maria ruminated that it all had come to look like self-centeredness best explained Tony more than any high or low or addiction *du jure*.

Then she laughed at herself.

His very self-centeredness was what made him a great frontman for the Tony Silvio Project. There was a fun magnetism that made an entire stadium lock eyes with him and then his outsize personality, or mood, or whatever filled the arena. Maria was certain until now that she'd never find another man like him. Another ride like this.

When she went down this thought path, she wanted him to make amends because she wasn't ready to admit defeat and cut her losses. Like the Tracy Chapman song that begged, "*Give me one reason to stay here.*" Like the Mary Cheever poem "*Gorgon*" that Maria understood too well, trading your own life for the prismatic colors of the Tony Silvio Project and the draining drunk at its core. Maria knew women like them would understand that the only way to withstand Tony's excesses and excuses was to harden yourself to a stone monolith like the Gorgon.

But this last fight had done it for her. He had made another confession, that part was not so new. She had learned over the years, thanks to several couples counselors, to remind herself that at least he was coming clean, at least she was hearing it—whatever it was—from Tony directly. This time was different though. The other confessions were more confirmations of her suspicions. They were admissions that her accusations were right.

This time she got a shock that flipped the script on everything she thought she could still hold onto about them. Until now she saw their union as a romance that was holy, something in which at their core they were both innocent and could return to time and time again. They might sully it with her anger or his using, drinking, and debting. But they had that one crystal of purity they could polish off and return to.

She had been wrong in this, wrong all along. It turns out that a few days before Tony asked her to be his wife, while they were on a tour stop in Boise, Idaho, he made another woman conceive.

During her engagement another woman carried his child. The child she and Tony were never able to have together was being carried by another. Some of her rage, Maria realized, was just that old ugly jealousy she felt from time to time toward women who were blessed with fertility. It was certainly also that powerless jealousy she felt toward the groupies, blaming them instead of blaming him—he was afterall the one who made the wedding vow to her. The part that killed her was that he hadn't even been faithful when their love was still young.

Something was different, something broke inside of her.

She did not feel the burning anger or shame or even hatred that she had felt in the past. She just felt done.

He seemed to brush over all that and instead urged her to meet what his cheating had spawned. "She's a young woman, raised in Pennsylvania by a farming couple. Her name is Jessica. She has brothers and sisters who were all adopted. What I did was wrong to you, but she's not wrong. If you met her, you'd actually see her as a sweet young girl."

"*I* was a sweet young girl! What about me? When does this end? One paternity suit wasn't enough?" That had been a long ugly chapter and it turned out he wasn't the father. But he could have been. It took a lab administering a test, doing something called "chain of evidence", and having an expert explain the results in court.

Tony answered her, but in a weary tone. "No one is suing about paternity. She has a mother and father. Cyrena named me, Bishop says her DNA test checks out, and to do the right thing by her I have to acknowledge I'm her birth-father."

"What about me? What about the timing, right around our marriage proposal?"

"It's not about you," he said somewhat dolefully.

"It never is," said Maria quietly.

"I kept it out of the book. They wanted me to put it in *The Birth of the True* but I told them 'No'."

Maria hated this tactic. He'd throw out one crumb like this and she'd have to fight against feeling guilty for not being grateful. She wasn't going to settle for that this time.

"Instead it's plastered over every entertainment show and website. Of course, the number of your social followers jumps tenfold when it gets 'leaked' strategically to the blogosphere.

Was that your idea or the idea of that 'sweet young girl' of yours?"

"That stuff just gets out there, you know that. She—Jessica—didn't leak it."

"Well, I guess you've got *her* back," Maria snapped with fierce pain.

Tony looked surprised. Maybe he was still expecting Santa Maria. He didn't answer her. The silence was the worst. He had no idea how she felt and maybe didn't care, Maria wasn't sure.

Maybe all she'd been all these years was the foil, the rube he made a fool of even hours before he proposed. The whole band must have known. Maybe that was the point. Just falling in love and staying in love wasn't enough. Just creating, performing and holding an audience, the things she loved about him, weren't enough. Maybe he always needed to have a victim by his side. She would have loved to storm out, loved to go to the media herself, but that just wasn't her.

Something needed to change. She couldn't just accept him and accept his taking her for granted again.

She would wait it out until he changed or until she changed enough to leave without looking back. To do that, Maria realized, she needed a change of scenery.

She caught a red-eye to Madrid where she'd grown up.

Her mother and sisters were still in Spain. She thought like a true American who refers to her family in Europe, or Africa, or Asia as "still" being there, as though it were only a matter of time before everyone came *here*.

These flights manicured night so its New World sunset was

followed at a surreally brief clip by sunrise over the pines of the central Iberian Peninsula.

So many years when her husband Tony was on the road and she knew things and didn't know. Times even when she'd returned from Spain after seeing her family for a few weeks. When she came back, he wasn't always hungry for her. He seemed to be sated already. This in itself added a certain suspense, Maria told herself.

* * *

Tony stopped in a high arched doorway with a realization: he loved Maria. It was one of those old realizations that flooded back now and then. What was new was the understanding that he might be falling *in* love with her just as she might have finally fallen *out*. The hallway seemed to echo with no sound.

He walked to their empty master bedroom. Tony noticed his own heartbeat as he remembered Maria turning the knob. It was when she was about to make one of her entrances from her dressing room. There were actually two doors, one at her private dressing room, then after a high passage only a few feet long, the final doorway to their chamber. When they bought the place Maria had this last one removed and replaced with a curtain of beads she found in Morocco. The two steps down from the passageway into their lair below added to the effect. The first time she stepped from the backlit passage he watched the strings of beads part over her Raphaelite hair. He loved when a strand or two slid over the rise of her breast or lingered across a glow of her thigh before disappearing behind her haunch with a sound like a brush on cymbals.

One evening when Maria wore Czech tasseled pasties and the Thai gold leaf tattoos, he laughed out loud with anticipation. Her foot hesitated. He thought the gesture was vestigial modesty from his Vestal Virgin, until he noticed a bejeweled toe ring. Tony began talking her to him with a low seductive banter and she looked at him anew, momentarily surprised. Her lips parted and she took a leisurely step closer to him.

She truly had a beautiful back, too. One of the prettiest sights in his entire life was lying flat on his back looking up at her moving shoulder blades and hips as she straddled him. She'd managed to keep her suede cowgirl hat on the whole time. He knew he'd been a good boy when she pulled it off and turned to toss it on his chest while shaking loose her curls. Her silhouette as she twisted toward him was its own reward.

Sometimes she liked it dark and he would find their bed by the light of a single red incense stick.

On other moonless nights she wore strands of frankincense that perfumed the spaces between their kiss.

Then there was what Tony thought of as the marriage thing. The warmth and fullness of her beneath the sheets, still asleep in the morning. Sometimes in a single glance or gesture Tony could read Maria in all her ages: the child, the wild girl, the curvy woman, even the earthly mother and the sage spirit. This last one—he didn't usually like to think about growing old—but Maria would be the kind to wear colors and cool baubles while sharing an apothecary of mystical herbs and medicinals.

In the fullness and ripeness of her apothecary—Maria's word—he recalled the rose petals that release their perfume as they bruise under their knees in bed. He recalled the tumble of lilacs she tossed on the gauze canopy and the striking firmness of a single waiting lily on his nightstand.

He realized how much Maria meant to him, how much he missed her. He prayed he had not lost her for good, but he did not know how to tell her. The sadness filled his heart.

* * *

Doors to this museum in Madrid, so very *madrileño* in their soaring height and svelteness like the shutters watching over the *travesias* and *calles*. The sounds we make for colors, thought Maria, are themselves so pretty: *rosé, malva* and *amarillo.* The names were warm and lustrous.

There was a picture, "Church Tower in Cordoba", that reminded her of the climbing geraniums in the Miraflores neighborhood of Lima. She had traveled there with Tony when he played there once, a private party, its orange trees dark and fruited along the white plane of its courtyard.

Maria was drawn to some ecclesiastical paintings she remembered from her last visit here years earlier. There was the delicate "*Moises selvado de las aguas*", Moses saved from the bulrushes. Maria pushed aside thoughts of the existence of Tony's newfound daughter, a Moses returned from Egypt. Instead her eyes rested on the oil brushstrokes of grays on grays, painted in the Flemish colony of Spain by Orazio Gentileschi.

These pictures were making her wonder about the adoptive father of Tony's biological daughter. Tony hadn't mentioned that man. Maria spotted two portraits of Joseph by Anton Rafael Mengs. Until this morning she had never thought of Saint Joseph as an adoptive father. Now she gazed at one of the portraits where Saint Joseph sat wearing a yellow garment and holding a staff from which white roses were sprouting.

A few light paces and she stood before "Saint Joseph with the Boy" painted in 1650 by Sebastian Martinez, again with Joseph in yellow, this time a cloak or blanket tossed over his shoulders as he held, again, a stick of white roses. Jesus is dressed in a violet tunic and is reaching for a bowl of fruit—a pomegranate, an apple, some grapes—Mary is nowhere to be found and instead it is his adoptive father who is chiding him not to play with the fruit.

Maria walked over to another, "The Sacred Family", this time by Francisco de Goya with light flooding the carpenter's workshop of Saint Joseph. *Tony had always wanted freedom, not family. She had always wanted Tony.*

In a third portrait, "The Holy Family with a Bird", Joseph was the center of the frame in a gray cloak with a curry-colored blanket on his lap. Mary was off to the side working at her spinning. The infant Jesus wore a sash and he and his adoptive father Joseph played together with a white puppy and a bird. Could Maria love Tony's child as Saint Joseph loved our Lord Jesus? Could Maria see Jessica and not see her groupie mother, just one of Tony's many betrayals?

The next room devoted an entire wall to Diego Velazquez' "La Meninas" with children, dwarves, rulers in a small mirror, the artist behind his easel. The children were larger than the king, as if to say more important to the portraitist than the king. She thought of Tony. She thought of their years together and still she would rather have a child than him, if forced to choose. Would she dare though?

The next was stylish. "Almond Trees in Flower" showed the sandy dirt road like the one she had walked yesterday with a girlfriend through *El Retiro*. The orchard in the foreground before a hedge of pines. Behind them the river. Then a spit of land lined with home smoke and sienna roof tiles facing the open sea. Maria longed for hearth smoke now, a child on her hip. Funny how those wants could beckon and become inconsolable needs.

Something darker in her drew her to a particular theme. An unformed thought led her from gallery to gallery where first she found "The Encounter Between Tamar and Judah" by Tintoretto, then "Abraham and Hagar" by Jan Mostaert in Haarlem. Their illicit love stories were caught in pale mauves and golden yellows that glowed from frames with patterns as ornate as storm clouds.

Finally she found the smaller gallery with the Arent de Gelders. It was just as Maria had remembered. De Gelders had been inspired to paint as many as five thick oils revivifying the tryst between Tamar and Judah. She ignored the scholarly wall notes that indicated some may have actually been painted by other artists. It was clear that the Flemish artist did not judge Tamar for her methods, and Maria did not judge Tamar or Judah either. Indeed the redolent lust of Tamar and Judah tugged at her low inside.

One time in their home she walked down a long corridor to follow the sound of furious whispering. She came to a door she knew she had left open. It was shut. She pressed her fingertips against it, a pair of spiders resting. By now the voice had cut off abruptly. She slid one hand down, palm against the door knob, grasped and turned it. The lights were off and the cold sweated down to her hands and stomach. A figure hunched in the dark.

Just as quickly she was flooded with a new kind of alarm when she heard.

"Maria?" It was preternaturally gentle. Silky. "Close the door, honey. It's just one of the engineers. This phone call's almost done. Close the door behind you. There. Good."

A woman? Drugs?

She liked to read biographies, always had. Marilyn Monroe. Kennedy. Chairman Mao. There had always been a genre within that genre, the rock memoir. It was more jagged: passionate unto chaos. In this sub-genre the protagonist often ended early and badly—Janis Joplin, Jimi Hendrix or Jim Morrison. The newest crop was autobiographical—as told to—with the ghostwriter capturing the celeb's fried voice in prose.

Hopefully the voice didn't rattle around too loudly in your cranium as it traced the inevitable arc from grubby garage band through excesses of sex'n'drugs'n'rock'n'roll to a beatific life after rehab. Sometimes that last rehab didn't take. Wash. Rinse. Repeat.

The girls like her, the girls with the band were usually blips. Collateral damage. She and Tony were something of a revelation because they stayed together. Married twenty-two years. Tony fifteen years sober. Or seven. Or two. Not yet solvent or serene. In those years he'd made plenty of confessions. Some were just acknowledging what she'd suspected all along. Sometimes she confronted him. A woman. A trove of bottles. A whispered bet. A delivery to the locked practice studio.

Sometimes she almost forgot them until one of his confessions jolted the memory back, and with it, the realization that a particular doubt or premonition had always been true. Until then she'd let herself half believe his labored explanations. Sometimes she made the excuses for him herself. But now, standing on her own on her home turf of Madrid, she was just weary of the whole charade and felt like she was done with the craziness of The Tony Silvio Project in her life.

6

It's Tricky

If you could keep your heart shielded, she reasoned, a casual affair could provide the antidote. *She* could be the one sneaking around. *She* could mix her horror at the wrongness of her decision and the outlandishness of the lies she would have to deploy. *She* would have the final, deep satisfaction of knowing what it was like to have the upper hand. *She* could be the one outside on the town, finally having her senses titillated in the way that virtuous steadfastness to Tony didn't provide.

Years back she had screamed—screamed herself hoarse—at either his latest hangdog confession or his latest insultingly sloppy lie.

And then he smirked.

"You're insufferable," Maria had said.

Tony's eyes danced.

It suddenly occurred to her that watching the enraged wife was *part of* the adrenaline rush for him. He got something out of it.

Yet she stayed.

After that particular fight a couple years ago, he really did clean up. He bought her a mama and baby goat for their Hudson valley farm. They fed them together and he held her hand. He lifted her chin between his calloused thumb and finger, gazing at her with such sincere love. That look in his eyes was true.

As Maria and Tony returned to quieter times, when they were closer, he insisted that his smirks were a nervous grimace.

She loved him. When her girlfriends asked her why, she struggled to give examples, "There's no one I'd rather go shopping with. Maybe I'm hooked on being with the band and if I wanted perfect adherence to the golden rule, I'd have married a gardener."

She forgave him.

And yet one thing remained: she wanted to be ravished, to forget all this effort at forgiveness. She wanted physical joy.

* * *

The stranger she met in the *tapas* bar was laughing at her joy, her anticipation. She was laughing for that and something else. A ribbon of true merriment at herself. She was aroused even by the smell of his leather vest. She fingered it.

She loosened the nubby silk of his tie. It was real raw silk; she could tell because it smelled like pumpkin the way the pure silk always does. His freshly shaved chin brushed her forehead as he grabbed her with open palms around her hips. The wool of his academic's blazer. Wool, silk, leather, she was already floating away on her senses yet she was sure she hadn't even smelled a pheromone yet.

Later, in their room she gasped with expectation as he slid

one hand gently to her lower back. She heard him slide his belt off the corduroy pants, a soft zip sound, then the clinks of his buckle hitting the rug near their bare feet.

The last fully formed sentence she remembered thinking was, "Finally this again, I deserve *this*."

The next weekend she found herself walking along the ocean of Donostia-San Sebastián arm in arm with her sister. They took a turn down by the quaint town along the waves.

The light was always whiter at sea level, as though an oceanic hand had soap-washed the streets, the buildings, the signs. Instead of divine detergent though, the cottages along this strand of the northern coast of Spain smelled of salt. There was lightness to the scent as fair as girls' cotton dresses, young men's linen sleeves. The wine at the sidewalk café where they took seats was white or rose in crystal carafes, proffered on fine silver trays.

Memory was as thin here. Tony with his dalliances, or any love child, were beyond those waves. The centuries heavy with war, or more recently collaboration and Franco, were let go: a tulle scarf carried out of reach on a breeze. History was nothing more, the afternoon was new. Yet Maria confessed to her sister, Lourdes, and told her his name: Elias.

Though Elias was not by her side now, her eyes still danced with the near memories of his intoxicating halo of confectionary glances, touches and endearments. Maria's elder sister listened somberly, then rose to steer them back to the cobbled street that in turn led them to the gracefully curved steps up to the family's rented cliff-side villa with its topaz pool.

Her sister and mother got them an invitation the next week-

end to the courtyard gardens between two villas in the hills beyond San Sebastián. Their hosts were away and once the three
of them, Mama, Lourdes and Maria, walked through a high
trellis of wisteria they found themselves in what was called the
blue garden. It lay before them enchanted.

The walk was lined with flowering purple spires of catmint
from the Caucuses. A few steps and they were looking down at
spikes of garden sage with tight blossoms the color of bruised
carbon paper. The border beneath them was soft with gray
lamb's ear. Maria stooped down and she felt the sun on her
shoulders through her soft woven shirt and remembered the
touch of his unfamiliar fingers there. Meanwhile Mama
pointed out the greenery that would burst later into nosegays
of forget-me-nots and bachelor buttons. Then Maria stood up
and gently took her mother's strong but mottled hand. Terra
cotta pots of johny-jump-ups and borders of deep azure and
purple pansies stood at the opposite side of the slate path that
meandered across a silvered lawn of sedge.

For a moment, still holding her Mama's fingers, she day-
dreamed that it was she and Elias that meandered arm in arm to
a wide, gentle set of flagstone steps. There a raised bed held an
alpine garden just below shoulder level. Much of its rockwork
was carpeted with varieties of smooth succulent leaves.

Lourdes seemed eager to explain that the owners were
known for their success with these tiny plants called *nana*.
Nana were culled from remote cliffs on each continent.

Juniper nana grew in plump whorls of needles no larger
than rosettes of moss. Another kind of nana, *globularia cordi-
folia*, made a cool, dark carpet of wedge-shaped leaves folded
closed as though in prayer. The prettiest nana were tiny deep

pinks, called *arenaria* with five flat miniature petals brightening to pastel near their stamens. They flung themselves up alongside silver white wisps of leaves. In patches around them grew stone cress that had tight cascades of cushion thick leaves, five petaled flowers that were yellow but flatter and floppier than buttercups, all grown round and waxy with water under the beating sun. Their blue gray spearheads reminded her of a salt marsh plant called sea orak from childhood vacations near Portugal. By summer's end its soft efflorescence would stand in salt water all the while starved for fresh water. Starved like a marriage to a rock star.

The sun raised the old-fashioned laundry soap smell from her collar. She never came across that smell in *Los Estados Unidos*. The same Spanish smell of soap clung to Elias' linens. She remembered how one of his large palms pressed her back closer to him, both she and he warm and beating at their cores, their very own inflorescence.

Just then a breeze blew in again off the sea, rustling her wrap between her legs, touching it tightly to her thighs. Maria imagined Elias there noticing, his eyes lingering on the dark triangle beneath her white fabric, as he held one of the French doors open for her to pass inside.

Instead she took supper with Mama and Lourdes on a table they carried out to the courtyard. When the meal was done, they poured each other another glass of madeira and sat as darkness rose from the west to face a full moon.

Both night and moonbeams cast across night blooming jasmine buds. Their unfurling was languid under a full moon. They were open, for quite some time, before she with her beloved elder sister and their mother left the garden.

She should call Tony. A call was long overdue. But instead she stood at the telephone table in the hall, tracing the grain of its wood sensuously and gazing back at the garden imagining Elias walking over to the jasmine. Maria's legs grew weak but she felt more peace than she had felt in years. She conjured, in no hurry, his shoulders and strong neck, his narrow hips, the way he moved, as he plucked the milky petals. Then he would step toward her and bend down. One of his strong, warm hands would peel away the cowl of her dress' neckline delicately. He would cup one of her breasts gently for only a moment before letting the aromatic jasmine petals fall into her bosom. Her cheeks burned and she let out a gasp.

Then with breathtaking slowness, gazing into her eyes, he would take enough time to make sure she felt what he wanted her to feel.

Her hand moved up to the telephone receiver but she let Elias' romantic ghost finish his words to her: 'Let me taste them again,' Elias would say, 'your lips are so red and full.'

The grass would be as warm as a bed. And then they would taste each other so exquisitely there again. She sighed and slid her hand off the receiver before either her Mama or Lourdes could interrupt. She hurried upstairs to her room to slide between the cool sheets and continue her reverie.

* * *

The message in Spanish was the same. All Tony knew was Maria hadn't phoned in five days. Now that he was trying to call her, he couldn't reach her. He keyed in the number for his mother-in-law again who used rapid Spanish and rushed him off the phone.

With Maria out of the house away in Spain, Tony had a freaky flashback of their life together as told through the rooms of their mansion. For starters, it had seven bathrooms. As a housewarming gift one of the guys in the band sent a whole case of toilet paper. The house itself was its own Kama Sutra of settings where he had made love to Maria. Tony pictured stop action of "The Wheel" in the sunken tub, "The Swing" up in the belvedere tower, and "The Two Palms". There was the winter she introduced wax and candles or the summer of ice and inflatable slides. Early on he was into buying her lingerie she seemed to enjoy. She wore it well anyway. She introduced him to high thread count sheets, rose lighting and love pearls.

Then there was the bonus of what Tony thought of as the marriage part. When they'd been physically apart too long or simply too mindlessly familiar for too long, it was a way to connect. Tony smiled and still remembered with pride how he'd blown Maria's mind by asking to buy her a flannel nightgown together.

"Tony, don't tease me!" Maria said. She was truly shocked. This couldn't be what it seemed. But it was. He liked the shell buttons down the front of the yoke. The laced shirring, the cheerful pattern. None of it hid her curves. You could rub its folds and find a waist of deep warm curves. Press in a little closer and be treated to a tight nipple and that inaudible but felt crunch of pubic fur. The softness of her skin radiated to him even before he lifted the hem and felt her flank. It was only a prelude.

Lingerie, too, was always only a prelude to that blessed feel of skin on skin.

He was still full of the memory and wanted to linger there but a certain jittery longing was pulling him. He took a deep breath. He had to acknowledge that something stank here, not hearing from her, not being able to reach her. *What was that phrase? Something is rotten in the state of Denmark.* He breathed it in, psychic smelling salts.

Yet, despite his best efforts, Tony could feel that old anxiety starting to twist in his stomach like a wet gray rope. He tried to hold fast to one thought, staying calm, but he found that his brain was buzzing like a thousand angry bees, his eyesight foreshortened, tension building at his temples.

Far from breathing in deeply and calmly, his diaphragm was tightening and his breath was becoming short and staccato. This was a dangerous place for Tony; he sensed a distant but insistent small voice inside saying how just one small drink would calm him down.

Another part of him wanted to just run like he used to, feel free and in control of his own life, not tied to Maria or anyone else.

A fast trip to All Saints in SoHo—he loved their black leather jackets—dinner at Le Bernadin or maybe Ko, call in a few friends like the old days. Hell, if Maria was on a tear, well, no one could match Tony Silvio in that department.

The rapidity with which this all ran through his brain, and, even worse, how right it sounded to him, scared the hell out of Tony. He stared at his gaunt face in the mirror and considered how deep his insecurity really was. *Maybe one of his sponsors,*

NA, AA or DA, would have an idea what to do. Forget the party. It was time to pick up the phone.

7

~

The Club

The PR officer for one of the largest law firms in New York, Dallas and LA stood in the Executive Conference Room announcing to a gathering of about two dozen men, "I think Clay should be our spokesperson. He's already used to the cameras from his years as a corporate officer."

As she continued, a senior partner of the firm, Ted Landtsman, carefully watched the men he had recruited for this effort who now stood crammed into the golden teak-paneled conference room.

Ted was preparing to represent a landmark case before the U.S. Supreme Court that would open a pandora's box for the adoption, surrogacy and artificial reproductive technology or ART industries, and these men were central to his strategy.

In state after state, where legislation was proposed to open up sealed birth records, ART and adoption industry lobbyists were arguing that people who were donor-conceived or adopted—and their descendants—should be identified as a separate class within society and denied access to their original birth certificates or that their birth certificates should be falsified to depict industry customers or 'intentional parents' as the DNA parents. No exceptions. This included no exceptions even for appeals for emergency family medical information or lifesaving bone marrow donors.

The lobbyists used a privacy argument as supposedly defending birth-mothers' rights to remain anonymous. The industry had to scrap that approach when too many birth-mothers came forward to testify that they had never been promised nor wanted privacy from their own children. A headline went viral that screamed, "You don't forget someone you carried in your body for nine months."

The lobbyists found themselves on the wrong side of history as more and more states unsealed adoption and donor documents to the people most entitled to them, the adult adoptee or donor-conceived person, while still maintaining reasonable privacy from everyone else.

Industry lobbyists turned instead to creating a slightly new cause. They still would attack and try to reverse what were named birthright laws. Birthright laws restored or recognized that adopted-out, fostered-out, and donor-conceived people had the same birthright as everyone else to know the name of both DNA parents, both genetic lines and families.

This legal tact went that while birth-mothers, whether willingly or under duress, had signed documents to relinquish their infants and therefore had a reasonable expectation that they would become known to their child(ren) or grandchild(ren), most birth-fathers had signed no such document. In fact, businesses offered some sperm donors a "no contact option" that vaguely was meant to bind their offspring in perpetuity under the terms of the donor payment.

Therefore, the argument went, birth-fathers had a right to privacy from—unless they explicitly agreed to be contacted—their DNA daughters and sons. The industry was determined to maintain secrecy. First the industry group hired a phallanx of lawyers. Then their next step was recruiting an anonymous sperm donor and a birth-father whom they would claim to be defending. Finally, the industry went public and filed a lawsuit asking for an injunction against birthright equality laws on behalf of the two anonymous fathers, John Doe 1 and John Doe 2. Kids on TikTok quickly nicknamed them SpermJoe and DeadbeatDoe.

Ted decided that the best way to prevent the creation of a separate class like this based on origin was to kill the privacy argument once and for all.

He realized that rather than try to wage this battle on a state-by-state basis, he was going with the strategy of taking a test case to the Supreme Court. Just like the champions of marriage equality had taken a test case to the Supreme Court. New York's legislature had overturned the secrecy laws yet the industry was mounting a rearguard action. He'd be damned if he let them.

The state-by-state battles would continue in the mean time. And now the "free states" outnumbered the industry states. A victory at the highest level, though, might speed reform, might set a precedent that would lift almost a century of imposed shame.

Ted had his PR staff place ads recruiting birth-fathers. He

would have them testify, as birth-mothers had earlier, that they claimed no right to "privacy" from their kids. It wasn't the only argument the legal team had. But it was the one with a face for the cameras.

Whatever the outcome in the lower courts, Ted knew either the industry would appeal, or, if the trial judge ruled on the wrong side of history and in favor of secrecy and lies, then *Ted* would appeal. He didn't come this far to come this far.

His PR team handed tablets out to the room and the PR officer continued, "I saw this interview clip with Clay Dennen on social. It was about opening adoption records. The first battle to restore adoptee access to their records has been won but the injunction is still in play. Clay was on message and has the right gravitas."

Indeed, Clay Dennen had been a C-level executive for many years, and it showed in the interview that appeared on screens around the room. He spoke in the clear, confident yet companionable tones of a seasoned leader, his tidy white hair and comfortable manner quietly establishing his "executive presence". Clay was exactly the front man that Ted Landtsman was looking for when he placed the ads.

The various birth-fathers and paralegals were still watching their tablets when Clay himself spoke up, "I'm humbled by all the praise, but you may be able to get someone with a lot more sizzle than me."

There was an expectant silence.

Clay smiled and put his glass down, "You've heard of Tony Silvio, right?" He tapped a coffee table with his index finger on each syllable as he said, "I know him."

"THE Tony Silvio?" asked Ted, and then without waiting for an answer he smiled his thousand-watt smile saying, "Yes, pretty good band. He has some memoir out this—it was in the Entertainment section, *Birth of the True*, I think it's called."

A few of the dozen people in the suite looked at each other.

The communications director spoke up, "You're referring to the story that he has a child out there who was placed for adoption, right?"

"Seems to be an occupational hazard for pop stars," one man joked.

Clay smiled but then looked at the communications director seriously, "I can't see him sitting at this group. Not yet, at any rate. But he's a neighbor. And I think I may be able to convince him to sign on."

"That could be a real stroke of luck," she said with genuine appreciation in her voice. "How well do you know him?"

"My wife knows his wife Maria pretty well. When I see him at the bottom of his road we wave, and we have a nodding acquaintance when we meet at the Club. Never really spoken to him much but he might be a resource. On the one hand he's 'busy' but on the other, if the hearing delivers a large enough audience, it might be a good venue for him."

Another birth-father named Martin jumped in and shot at Ted, "If you subpoena him doesn't he have to show up?"

"We only need friendly witnesses," Ted answered abruptly, resenting the intrusion.

Clay might be bringing him a better witness than he could have hoped for. Clay was someone he could work with. Ted could also make Clay the main contact with other birth-fathers so he wouldn't have to deal directly with personalities like this Martin.

Martin was still talking with something of the air of an insider, "Like you said, we could get him to come here at Ted's office, he's trying to sell his book anyway. This would be great for him, great for the case. Celebrities always need exposure, you know."

Ted rolled his eyes and started strategizing in his mind how best to get Tony Silvio on board.

* * *

About a week later the opportunity presented itself. Clay saw Tony Silvio on the veranda overlooking the country club's pool. Even though Tony Silvio was wearing sunglasses, Clay recognized him.

Tony Silvio had no clue who the executive type was walking over to introduce himself. Pretty quickly though Tony would know whether to be rude or charming.

Clay anticipated that music stars were approached all the time by people with business propositions, so he had come up with a quick statement, what they called an "elevator speech" in the corporate world. An elevator speech was how you'd describe your pet project in case you ran into a higher up while on the elevator. There you only had two or three floors to make your point.

"Look, I was reading about your memoir in the *Star-Ledger*, and I think we have something in common. I hardly look like your typical fan, though, eh?" Clay let out a self-deprecating chuckle and Tony noted Clay's white tennis shirt stretched over a small paunch tucked into blue "dad" shorts.

Clay continued, "C'mon, let's sit down and have a quick drink. I promise you it will be worth it."

Tony's back stiffened and he pulled his shoulders back as he considered the offer, then turned his head left and right as if looking for a way out of this conversation. Clay was waiting for just this moment.

"Somewhere out there I have a kid who I have never met. Don't know his name or even what he looks like. I walk the dog at night wondering if he's awake somewhere, or—"

Clay's voice dropped down, wet with emotion.

"—or if he's even alive."

Tony took off his sunglasses although the midday glare hadn't dimmed. Maybe something to keep his large-knuckled hands busy.

Clay had him, "I, we, admire your courage. I was touched when I read how your birth-daughter contacted you, how you two have been getting to know each other, and I just wanted to tell you how inspiring it is for me—and for all the other birth-fathers out there—to hear about. Telling your story in public will make it easier for us, I hope."

"Wow, man, just...wow."

Tony said it quietly. He had not given much thought to the fact that there were other birth-fathers out there who were not as lucky as he was to have found their kids. Jessica's smiling face popped into his mind and he almost smiled at the memory, but caught himself in time.

He did not want Clay to think he was laughing at his pain. All the other birth-fathers Tony had heard of were like Tony

Silvio, dudes in the limelight. It never occurred to Tony that there were guys like Clay out there who were completely unrelatable until now. Tony could now relate to this suite-with-a-commute! As usual, Tony Silvio had been so consumed by his own story and reunion with Jessica that he did not consider what was happening to other people. He could hear his AA sponsor saying to him, *"Ding, ding—that's your Higher Power sending you a wake-up call, a chance to give service to someone else in pain."*

One thing Tony was starting to learn was that doing Step 12 of his recovery program, reaching out to others who could use the support, was not limited to only alcoholics or drug addicts, folks in one of his programs. Service was service, and pain was pain, and if he could help someone regardless of the source, then it would help his own recovery as well, funny as it seemed.

"What did you say your name was? Clay, right?"

Clay nodded.

"Clay, man, yah, let's sit and talk a bit. That would be good. I want to hear more of your story."

Clay called over one of the attendants for an order of drinks and they moved over to a table under an umbrella. Clay noted with interest that the rock god ordered ginger ale on the rocks, twist of lemon.

Tony listened as Clay quickly summarized the story from years ago: his buying a little house for them when he found out his girlfriend was pregnant; the broken engagement; and, quick on that the news that the baby would be given away.

Tony, maybe a little improbably to some, after years of sitting in church basements filled with recovering addicts giving their shares, had gotten good at actively listening to tales of loss and powerlessness. They came from all walks of life.

"I mean, here I am, a man of influence in my career, someone who people treated carefully and who knows how to get what I want. But back then I was stunned into submission. I feel like I should have spoken up, asserted my rights as the father. But that was not how things happened back then, and her father, the Admiral, was far too strong for me to buck. He had the whole thing tied up with a legal bow before I even knew what hit me. I sold our little newlywed home. I'd bought us our own cottage. But by then it was too late. Or so I thought."

Clay paused in his story, looked intently into Tony's eyes, and realized that the rock star was still with him.

Tony cannily noted the old executive was slipping into his deal closing routine.

"Look, I said it was too late, but it turns out that may *not* be the case anymore for a whole lot of other birth-fathers out there. You see, there is this whole movement for countries, sometimes state-by-state or province-by-province, to make it easier for donor-conceived people, adoptees, and their descendants to find DNA family. Have you heard anything about this?"

Tony slowly shook his head no, then said, "I really don't know much about that stuff. My daughter, Jessica, she found me through DNA, I didn't even know she existed."

Clay nodded and started unspooling Ted Landtsman's legalese in plain English for Tony Silvio.

"For years the adoption and egg donation industries argued that opening records would violate the promise of anonymity made to birth-mothers or egg donors. But so many birth-mothers came forward to say that they were never promised anonymity—and don't want it—that the industry has been on a losing streak. Hell, Tony, the British Isles have had open records for decades and they're still floating. But here in the States the industry and all its lawyers have been fighting open records tooth and nail for years. Some states have passed laws restoring access, but many have not."

Clay paused for Tony's reaction.

"Following."

"Okay, so some smart lawyers on *their* side came up with a new tack: claiming they were protecting a birth-*father's* or male donor's right to anonymity."

Tony snorted at that.

"Anonymity? Hell, I had no clue I even HAD a kid out there. No one promised me anything. The mother, Cyrena, she never even told me."

"Exactly. Many birth-fathers were never told about the pregnancy, or they were not told they had any parental rights to give up in the first place."

"Right, Jessica said something about that to me. TPR or something."

Clay smiled.

"'Termination of parental rights.' Your daughter knows her stuff. You, me, so many of us, we did not even get to sign a paper saying we relinquished our rights to be parents. We were supposed to. We were just an adjunct to the process, love 'em and leave 'em, spreading our wild oats and all that."

"Um, in my case that was probably true."

"Well, it doesn't mean you had to give up your rights. Who

knows, maybe you would have married the mom, or raised the kid."

An image popped into Tony's mind of raising Jessica with Maria. Would she have raised someone else's kid? Well, it was his kid also. He felt like maybe this was another missed opportunity in his life. Clay was still talking.

"So, Tony, me and a bunch of other birth-fathers are working together to try to fight against that industry argument. We are saying that no one asked us birth-fathers, and that we want birth records opened for all adoptees and donor-conceived people so that they can find their heritage, their birth-mother *or* birth-father more easily. We call ourselves The Birth-Fathers' Club."

"LOL, you mean like *The Breakfast Club*? I saw that when I was a kid!"

"Yah, like that, only more focused and strategic. We are working with a major New York law firm with a huge lobbying presence, and we are about to take on our first court case where the industry has sued to stop an open records law that was recently passed. And that is where *you*, with your high-profile reunion, can help." Clay's demeanor and somber tone precluded even the rock'n'roller from dismissing him easily. Clay dropped his voice again and began laying it out for Tony quickly: they wouldn't initially advertise his presence among the witnesses; anonymity was a given for this so-called Birth-Fathers' Club idea of Ted's.

Finally, the quid pro quo, thought Tony.

"Word will probably get out after the first meeting. This could be excellent timing for the Tony Silvio Project. I know you know what I mean. For either the summer concert tour or the fall book tour."

Tony laughed. Tony agreed with Clay that his attendance would be a draw.

"You sure did your research. Then again, my whole life seems to play out on the Internet these days, sometimes before I even know about it! Basically, me being a spokesperson, if you will, could get the Birth-Fathers' Club off the ground just by itself!"

Tony Silvio could see that those words made Clay hopeful. Tony took a sip from his drink and spread his legs out in front of his chair. "Soon after my first album was released, I found out that even something as simple as taking the subway turns into a crazy, craven, cracked autograph session."

Tony was enjoying taking his time, keeping this suit waiting as he doled out his words slowly.

"I learned the hard way to avoid unchoreographed sessions with strangers, you know?"

Clay nodded reassuringly, "Security would be in place. I've been an Executive Vice President for years and I understand overexposure. I completely get it—"

Tony grinned at Clay, guessing that senior executives might know a little bit of what it was like.

Clay, too, broke into a smile. He knew he had this and so he reached forward to shake Tony's hand, to seal the deal.

Tony Silvio leaned forward too. Then Tony looked him straight in the eye and gave him an answer.

"No."

Clay probably was not used to being told "no" and for a sec-

ond some annoyance seemed to cross the chiseled face and settle in his shoulders. Tony watched the distinguished man in the
tennis whites sit back and consider this flat rejection.

Once upon a time the "old Tony", as he liked to think of
himself before recovery, would have leapt into Clay's fight simply for the thrill of doing something new, of sticking it to an
amorphous industry, and to keep his name in the headlines.
Truth be told, he still got a thrill out of seeing his face on the
cover of those rags when he was at the grocery store—as well as
the incredulous looks he received from cute cashiers when they
realized that the guy they were ringing up was mirrored in the
racks they stared at all day.

He found that the miffed look he got from Clay, the hesitation and calculation behind his strong gray eyes, was almost
as much fun as what he got from the clerks. Perhaps this saying
"no" thing might have legs after all.

Besides, Tony and Maria still weren't good on this whole
birth-daughter thing. There was still too much unspoken between them about Jessica, and he wondered if it might not be
such a good thing to give it too much public air time, not just
yet.

But Clay wasn't giving up.

"Listen, I appreciate your not wanting to be too accessible.
I've been in the same position in senior leadership in corporate.
But this isn't that kind of situation, Tony. You're not going out
there doing this on your own. We have a whole team of lawyers
and PR advisors and a bunch of other guys, like me, who are
standing up to tell the world that we are fathers and our kids
have a right to find and meet us. Or not, but it's finally their
call. Heck, a bunch of us never even knew we had kids out

there. Having someone of your public stature, Tony, testify for us would be a huge lift to our cause. You would be helping hundreds of kids reunite with their birth-fathers, if they want to, just like yours did."

The last point had hit home and Tony took a deep breath. Then he took a deeper pull on his ginger ale and looked out over the golf course. There were cumulonimbus clouds bunching in the near distance and heading their way. The two men sat quietly like that for a long while, Clay allowing Tony's thoughts to go where they may, the old sailor sensing that the wind had turned in his favor. Time to try again to inch toward that deal.

"Look, you've got an agent, I'm sure. Run this by him. I have a feeling he'll see the symbiotic opportunity here. We could help you and you could help the cause. A classic win-win situation, Tony."

"Ah—"

"Sorry, I don't mean to put you in the middle here. Let me speak to him directly. What's his name?

"Clay, you've done enough, I got it, man. He's calling me Friday; I'll mention it to him. I don't even know where he's got me booked for. Let's just see where this all might fit, okay?"

Clay smiled. They both stood up as they shook hands.

Clay, in spite of himself, felt a bit in awe as he firmly squeezed the hand that had launched a hundred tunes. This was how Clay always ended such conversations, with a warm but solid grip, a look straight into the eyes, and an unspoken message that he was confident that they would continue to work to their mutual benefit.

He just hoped that the message would carry through to

Tony when he spoke with his agent on Friday. It wasn't the commitment Clay was aiming for but he held out hope that Tony Silvio's agent would buy into the Birth-Fathers' Club.

Tony got up and ambled away from the table. Even though this talk with Clay got him thinking about his being a birth-father in a much larger way, he still hated these unscripted encounters when Bishop wasn't around to whisk him away. Instead, Tony had to wait through Clay holding on just a moment too long when shaking hands.

He wondered where Maria was.

8

~

Park Avenue

Clay called Ted to report on the meeting with Tony, saying that he thought Silvio was leaning their way, but that he might need some more coaxing.

Ted was not willing to wait for Clay to play his hand out with Tony. He knew the value of having a rock star on board, and swung into action on his own.

With barely enough time to add Tony to the witness list, Ted had one of the paralegals go to a book discussion at Union Square to meet Tony Silvio on the autograph line for his rock memoir, *Birth of the True*. Ted chose her because she looked young enough to be the age of Tony's daughter, but also because she was going to law school at night and he knew that she had the bearing and verbal skills to make the case to Tony Silvio quickly and forcefully in the few minutes she would have with him at the bookstore.

As she later recounted to Ted, Tony was in his full-on rock'n'roller banter when she approached him at the table, calling her "sweetheart" and twinkling his eyes at her when asking who she wanted the book dedicated to.

Without missing a beat, she asked him to dedicate the book to all the adopted and donor-conceived people out there who were being denied access to know their own fathers or other paternal relatives.

Tony stopped with his pen in mid-air, looked up at her a bit suspiciously, and then she told him she was a fan but also worked with Ted and Clay and how they really needed birth-fathers to come forward as witnesses. She smiled and winked at him conspiratorially

She reported that Tony stared at her with amusement for a minute, and then said, "Well, darling, if they went to this length to drag me in, it looks like it might be worth my time to find out a bit more."

She handed Tony Silvio one of Ted Landtsman's cards, which Tony handed over to someone sitting behind him, who then promised he would reach out to Ted the next day. That must be Bishop, the handyman and fixer for the Tony Silvio Project, who went by the street name of The Glove.

The next day, Bishop did indeed call to set up a face-to-face with Ted. This thrilled Ted, not only for the strategic options this opened, but also because Ted always liked entertaining a Name. The Tony Silvio Project was a little after Ted's time but you couldn't have been alive in the past ten years without having "*Wedding Vow Hearts*" lodged somewhere in the back of your brain.

One cancellation and a reschedule later, Bishop led the Tony Silvio Project entourage up to attorney Ted Landtsman's glass-walled floor where coffee and Danishes were already waiting for the few moments they would stand there. No one in the entourage seemed surprised and a roadie who had been invited along helped himself.

Bishop was about to have the receptionist let Ted know Tony Silvio and his entourage had arrived. Instead, she rose immediately and brought them down a thickly carpeted hallway to a breathtaking conference room. When Tony Silvio walked in, Ted rose. A young paralegal appeared from a doorway, with no real purpose Tony could see other than to take in the scene. He was aware Ted was taking him in too.

Tony Silvio was tall, had stage presence, seemed at ease or could act it, and wore layers of what Ted would describe as art house clothing. Ted came around the table, took Tony's hand in both of his as he introduced himself and gestured to one of the leather chairs at the head of the teak and mahogany table.

He poured them both club soda from the crystal decanter set he received when he made senior partner. The paralegal stepped in and offered drinks to the rest of the group. Tony picked up a chrome gadget, a high-end puzzle maybe, preening for his posse then passing it around.

As the musician drank, Ted delivered some customized banter that started with the view of the city from the room's wraparound window and ended with the particulars of rock memoir sales and the relative standing of *Birth of the True* on the Times' Best Sellers list.

Ted watched for what he learned to call in poker a "tell". It could be anything from a glance tossed sideways, or a slowing of the hands, to a rolling of the shoulders. Actors learned to affect them for their characters but the average person didn't realize they even had them. The "tell" would let Ted know when he'd hit a sweet spot or when the musician was trying to cover something up.

When Ted next pointed out the state-of-the-art lighting in the office or how he had had this window installed, Tony exhaled as though preparing for a tedious ordeal before he deliberately widened his eyes to feign interest.

On the other hand, when Ted gestured for Tony to come look down at the city park below, people scuttling by under umbrellas like so many black beetles, Tony laughed with simple amusement. As Ted demonstrated the built-in speakers that were designed by a boutique engineering company Tony's reverent exclamations were genuine, if juvenile. When Ted inquired into ticket sales or download metrics related to the Tony Silvio Project, Tony stayed the musical purist who was too much of a rebel artist to care about, let alone divulge, numbers, adding a curt statement, "I leave that to the accountants."

But when Ted talked about the potential impact of the case on music and book sales, his wife Maria, or new-found daughter Jessica, the restless Tony seemed to transform once more. The overaged adolescent grew still and was replaced with a canny survivor who listened not only with his ears but with his pores as his hooded eyes seemed to be doing a calculus even Ted couldn't read.

Tony Silvio, surmised Ted, was a mix of untamable showman and adolescent enthusiasms hiding a seasoned midlife merchant and potential family man. The latter reassured Ted.

Tony returned to the table and sat down. Ted followed him and pushed a binder of papers across the table toward Tony. "I want you to take a look at these."

Tony Silvio sat back in his chair, not touching the portfolio in front of him.

"Whoa, Ted. Man, these are an inch thick. You edjucatin' me into some lawyer?"

"No, I'll handle the representation and the argument—the lawyering," said Ted wryly, adding with a hard look, "I think you know where you're key."

"With the ladies?"

Then Tony pulled down his shades and flashed brilliant blue eyes. Even Ted stopped and chuckled.

"No, you embody—your image for a lot of people—is about living for today, sowing wild oats, love 'em and leave 'em."

Tony threw his head back and laughed.

"Ted, we all, me, Mick, Keith, Steven Tyler, we all got kids out there somewhere. Spreadin' our seed as they say."

"Right, right. Exactly. So when you step up and testify that you actually do care about your birth-children, folks are going to sit up and pay attention. It's like Nixon going to China, Reagan to Reykjavik...."

Tony gave Ted a quizzical look to make him realize he needed to provide more context.

"Right, let me back up," Ted said, "You are going to be playing against type, telling us all that the truth is not what we think it is. That disconnect will make your story that much more compelling. By the way, have you ever testified before?"

Tony shook his head slowly, not as comfortable with that thought as he was being on a stage in the Meadowlands with tens of thousands of fans cheering him on. The thought of standing, no, sitting there alone, no guitar in hand, no supporting cast around him, clearly had him uncomfortable.

"Nah, man, I mean, I have met with lawyers before, done some depositions when we had to sue a record producer, but I ain't never testified in court or at a hearing, we always settled it out."

Ted sat up straight and looked confidently into the musician's eyes. "Listen, it's like this: I heard you and the band hired a blues singer at one point to teach you how to do that kind of riff, right?

"Sure, Amos Johnson. He was a musician's musician. Truth be told he shoulda been a fifth member of the band. We did pay Amos well though. I'll own it though: fifth member of the band. That's what we shoulda called him."

"Well, I don't know about Amos Johnson but we've got a chance now to set something else right. And for a whole lot more people than just one blues player."

"You don't need to sell me, man. I'm already on board, else I wouldn't be here. *Capice?*"

Ted caught the beginning of frustration in Tony's voice, so he rushed on, not wanting to lose Tony Silvio's attention, which was famously short. "Well, now for your testimony—I'm your Amos Johnson: I want to inject the authentic blues in this situation. Speak truth to the machine. The standard howdy-doody line is birth-fathers were just having fun, didn't want to spend their lives with the lady. Instead there's some nice middle-class couple out there, waiting for a kid, been together for years who would raise the kid right away. Fair enough as far as it goes, right?"

"But her eggs don't hatch or his boys don't swim!" Tony

grinned at the lawyer, proud that he could entertain even in this stuffy office.

Instead, Ted pulled a stern and sour face, pointed a finger at Tony, and said, "That's exactly the turn of phrase you are not using during testimony, right?"

"I'm salty but I'm no idiot: they get the baby and live happily ever after. Picket fence, golden retriever, and a ride-on lawn mower. The lady moves on with her life, gets married and has two new kids. Both birth-parents forget they even had a kid somewhere. No singing the blues by no one, we all got amnesia and live happily ever after. I got it."

"You got the party line. But you're missing the authentic blues here. Just follow me for a minute: you can fill stadiums but your own flesh and blood will not get a piece of it. You don't know how they're doing."

Tony suddenly looked up at the lawyer sitting across the coffee table from him. He was decked out in a bespoke worsted wool suit, brilliant white shirt, and striped silk tie. The guy may have been trying to talk like he was jive, but it was clear to Tony that this lawyer was more comfortable with complete sentences and cocktail parties than he was with Tony's world. And yet. There was an earnestness in Ted's voice that spoke volumes to Tony Silvio. Tony had been wondering why some high-priced Park Avenue lawyer was taking on the Birth-Fathers' Club as a client. Now Tony Silvio was thinking it might be more of a cause than a client.

"Yeah. I seen some bad shit."

"Exactly. Your firstborn is gone. She doesn't know anything about you—just that it was okay to give her away. Just that you never want to see her face again."

"That's bullshit," Tony was on his feet.

"But you see, Tony, most kids relinquished don't know that. All they know is that their birth-parents gave them away, they were unwanted. The State seals their records. Hides their birth certificate with your name and your girlfriend's name on it. And now the adoption industry is saying that's what you and she wanted in the first place and it would be a violation of YOUR rights to let your own kid see their own birth records," said Ted.

Tony paced back to the wall of floor-to-ceiling windows, back turned to the rest of the room. *If he had known back then, would he have wanted Jessica? He couldn't say, didn't matter, he knew from recovery that 'you're only as sick as your secrets' and these secrets were from a different time. What he would or wouldn't have done had he known about Jessica was one topic. What actually did happen was another.* He didn't turn around when he spoke, "That's just not true. Jessica said her birth-mother, Cyrena, was told to go away and not bother our kid's new parents. They told her it was the best thing, for the baby to be able to grow up in a solid family without having to worry about someone coming back for her." Then Tony turned to face Ted before continuing, "Me—hell, I didn't do nuthin'. Never even signed a paper. Never even knew Cyrena was pregnant or that Jessica was born."

Ted saw the hurt in Tony's eyes. Ted ventured, "You know, some things have changed a bit since your day. Today, if you were listed as the father, they'd have to get you to sign off. But you read the news: Cheesewhiz attorneys tell the mother to lie and say that she doesn't know who the father is. Then they whisk her off on a plane to a state where the adoption laws are loose. And, bam, just like that the father loses any right to raise his own kid, if he wants to. Family law is an animal unto itself, Tony, and this young generation that thinks they've resolved anything legally or psychologically with open adoptions are just going to be annuities for the next generation of lawyers and therapists."

"Annuities?"

"Sure. *Their* legal and therapy bills are going to pay for *our* vacation homes. I tell you, enforceability of any of these open adoptions will be a legal nightmare. The whole idea of open adoptions solving the problem is a figment of legal imagination. But the issue you and I are dealing with right now is to break open the records of kids like your daughter who were part of the 'Baby Scoop Era' when adoption records were definitively sealed. End of speech," Ted wrapped up.

"Ok, so we go into court and we beat them and force them to open their records?" Tony was warming up to the thought of testifying in an electric courtroom drama.

"Well, um, no, it is not quite like that, Tony."

Then Ted slid a coaster over before sitting down across the coffee table from performer.

"You see, in this case, the legislature has passed a law restoring access to original, truthful birth certificates for adult adoptees and donor-conceived people."

"I don't get it, man. If the law is already passed, then why are we talking about testimony and lawsuits here? *Are you wasting my time?!*" Tony Silvio was pissed. He watched, waiting, as Ted hurried to spread his hands soothingly.

"No, no, let me explain. Even though we were able to get the law passed in the legislature, the adoption industry is suing to get the law quashed. They want an injunction until a judge decides if the law is legal, in this case, whether it violates some guy's right to privacy if his kid finds him. They found an anonymous sperm donor and a birth-father to be fronts, to be the plaintiffs, but the industry is footing the bill. They've given us a test case. The legislative success already shows our cause is popular; now we have to show it's right. We will be creating case law that a right to privacy was never intended to create a class of people who based on the details of their conception lose their birthright to know where they came from."

Tony didn't hide his skepticism for all of Ted's legalism.

"Look, the new law is on hold because of this lawsuit. The judge said it could *not* go into effect. So, we are fighting them tooth and nail to get it kicked up as a civil rights issue before SCOTUS."

Tony threw back his head and burst out laughing, "That like scrotum?" He was happy to have something to fend off thoughts of Maria.

The attorney mustered as much gravitas as he could, "It's SCOTUS, Mr. Silvio, and it stands for Supreme Court of the United States."

The light returned to Tony Silvio's eyes. Now he was talking to the rest of his crew lounging around the conference room as much as he was this litigator.

"You're talking the sold-out concert tour of attorneys," Tony looked at Ted, "that's the *Madison Square Garden* for you guys, that's *live at Budokan*."

Tony got the appreciative laughter he was counting on from his entourage.

"With," said Ted, smiling proudly, "the *cachet* of the Kennedy Center."

Tony Silvio took his time striding back to the plush couch along one wall, eased in, and decided to take the message home for the rest of the room. "Ok, I get it. The law was passed but the industries are trying to get some judge to kill it. That's how they roll. Now we are going to get that law put back in action, right?"

Ted nodded appreciatively.

"Yup, that's it, in a nutshell. Tony, we are that close to giving others a chance at reunion, and we need your help." Ted leaned down to take the performer's glass, "Would you like another?"

"No, I'm ready. I'd like to get started on my statement."

Ted flagged the paralegal still standing in the doorway and just when they were about to begin, Bishop stepped in.

"Let's give the man some space. You got a lounge or something with screens where we can order up?" asked Bishop as the others started rising to their feet.

Ted called someone to set them up down the hall while Tony Silvio sat through a series of softball questions and answers with Ted over the next hour and a half.

After the celebrity was done, Ted made sure each member of the group left with swag usually reserved for their top tier retainer clients. Afterall, Ted was flattered to have this A-lister on his witness list.

Tony caught something out of the corner of his eye on the tablet of the paralegal who reappeared hovering nearby. It was a news story, a part of his past he'd just as soon forget, but he accepted that he wasn't ever going to live it down. At one of the

Tony Silvio Project's biggest tours, about fifteen seconds after taking the stage and taking in the roar of the fans, Tony fell off stage drunk into the orchestra pit. He never got back on stage during the course of the show that lasted over four hours while the rest of the band sang his tunes in unison—with a lot of instrumental—or just stood there jamming without him.

They must be figuring that with this deposition, if worse came to worst they would use Tony's statement today and have it marked into evidence if somehow the rock star fell off the wagon.

A few days later Tony ran into Clay again at the Club. Clay thanked him for the deposition but now had a second request, to talk to a boy in the neighborhood whose girlfriend was pregnant.

"Well, what do they want to do, the parents?"

"Well, the birth-father's parents—?"

"No, the boy is the father. He ain't no birth-father yet."

"He seems to be on the fence. Name's Dan."

Clay's wife, Ada, had asked him to get the Rock God to talk to the boy about consequences and late-to-the table fatherhood. What fan wouldn't listen to a sit-down on manning up if it came from Tony Silvio?

Meanwhile, *The Birth of the True* was getting as much buzz from the revelation that Tony Silvio was a birth-father as it was for its kaleidoscopic look behind the scenes at musical inspiration or storied partying.

9

~

Making It Through One Day

Tony was feeling antsy and uncertain for days when he suddenly looked up at Bishop and said, "I'm going to Rio, baby."

Bishop immediately understood the coded phrase, not that Tony was going to Brazil, although he had taken powders like that many times in the past to avoid stressful situations like breaking up with a girlfriend or relapsing in his AA or NA program.

No, the winking joke between them was that Tony was heading to the Ironbound section of Newark, New Jersey which was loaded with Brazilian and Portuguese restaurants and really good authentic *chacuteiras*. It was also where his sponsor in DA—Debtors Anonymous—lived and worked.

Tony Silvio met Fred at a 12 Step meeting close to ten years ago, and later Fred served on Tony's Pressure Relief Group meetings to help Tony Silvio dig himself out of a hole. Tony recalled the first time the PRG met together, Fred and some chick

(Diana, he could barely recall her face), sitting in the basement of an old brick church, the metal folding chair cold through his pant-legs. Tony had no idea what to expect, no clue how to start. All he knew was that his chest was tingling with anxiety and he was certain that the Tony Silvio Project was facing bankruptcy—which, by necessity as a Rock God, would be noisy and public and immensely embarrassing.

Right before then Tony had fired his third, or maybe his fourth, manager, and now these two volunteers were having him bring three paper bags full of bills and letters that he hadn't had the guts to open in months.

The three of them sat in a loose triangle around a folding table. Fred and Diana held out their hands and Tony realized they were waiting for him to join in. When they all held hands together, Tony felt a tingle of energy pass through him, a specter of hope. Fred and Diana closed their eyes, all were very quiet, and Tony's anxiety leapt into his throat again.

Were they waiting for him to do something, say something?

He cast about in his mind for some wise words to say, something deep and meaningful to meet the expectation, but all he found was confusion and fear.

Fred rescued him by quietly starting the Serenity Prayer—Tony knew that one from far too many AA meetings, and he slipped into the chant seamlessly along with them. But his mind was going in a million directions at once as he tried to focus on the words. *God, grant me the serenity to accept the things I cannot change, the courage to change the things I can, and the wisdom to know the difference.*

"So, what's pressuring you?" Diana asked.

Tony took a deep breath, then let go and it all tumbled

out—the creditors calling all day and night, not knowing how much he owed anyone, no clue about how much money he had coming in from anywhere, let alone if he had any money at all, getting rid of his last manager, the fear that he was going to be smashed by something he could not even see coming but knew was about to strike him down. He was completely buried in un-characteristic shame and details and could not see how it would ever get straight.

"Well, nothing like opening the mail!" Fred said brightly, pointing to the bags of unopened envelopes.

Tony wanted to kill him.

They spent the rest of the hour simply opening, reading, and sorting the bills from the other stuff, and a funny thing happened. By the end of the meeting a lightness settled on Tony, he had a glimmer of hope that he might see a way out of this after all.

Diana told him that the first step in recovery was to find clarity, to "track his numbers", to get a sense of what he had and what he owed in black and white numbers on paper.

They set up another PRG for the next week and told him to go home and start gathering more information and start writing down everything he spent, no matter how trivial, even when he gave a quarter to a homeless guy outside the recording studio.

Little by little it worked—over the next year Tony Silvio found clarity, serenity, and was on his way to being solvent for the first time in his adult life.

Tony Silvio liked the way that Fred was not intimidated by him or his fame, but instead treated him like any other guy who could not, to save his life, handle his debt or stop spending. After working together for a while in the PRG, Tony felt comfortable enough with Fred to ask him to be his 12 Step sponsor. Fred introduced Tony to Bishop who Tony Silvio hired when the next manager of the Tony Silvio Project quit. Fred, and then Bishop, might be the first people, other than Maria, who Tony had ever truly trusted in his life. It was still kind of scary.

It is amazing how much you can get away with when people expect you to be totally stoned out of your mind, Tony would muse. It is a built-in excuse for living over the edge, and as a rock'n'roll god he worked it for all that it was worth. He was like a superhero who lived by different rules from the rest of the world. People expected him to do insane things that no normal mortal could survive, and to keep on doing them despite all the wreck and ruin around him, and within him. But after years of getting straight in Alcoholics Anonymous, then Narcotics Anonymous, and Sex and Love Addicts Anonymous Tony realized that he still had not reached the real bottom of his compulsive itch. Finally in DA he started to really grow up and take responsibility for running his own life—with help from a Higher Power, "the God of my understanding", he reminded himself. He still forgot to thank "the God of my understanding" as often as his sponsor recommended.

Tony was remembering his entry into the DA program while standing, unrecognized, in front of St. Stephan's Church at the corner of Ferry Street and Wilson Ave here in the Ironbound. The Ironbound really was like walking into another place and time. Not only was it cut off from the rest of Newark by the elevated train tracks and truck depots that gave it its name, it was a cultural island unto itself where some streets had more Portuguese and Spanish signs than English.

Tony Silvio wore large dark aviator sunglasses and a Bruce Springsteen cap pulled low over his face, his typical outfit when he wanted to walk the streets unrecognized and un-hassled by fans. But when he was in the Ironbound he always felt like he could probably drop all that cover, prance around like the famous star he was, and still not be recognized by ninety percent of the folks on the street.

He doubted that many people around him even knew who Tony Silvio was, and when he showed up to spend some time with his sponsor that unusual anonymity felt right. He got to focus more on his recovery than on flaunting the famous Tony Silvio Project brand.

Tony Silvio, after so many years of meeting in church basements for various recovery groups, often gravitated to these singular edifices whenever he could. Not that Tony was religious in an organized sense. Really very little about Tony's life was organized in a traditional way and he either would not or, more likely, could not bring himself to participate in the ritual of religious masses. 12 Step meetings or face to faces with his sponsor were a different story. He always made those on time or early but there was no way that he could make it to a scheduled church service.

Yet also after so many years of invoking God in the Serenity Prayer and asking for strength from his Higher Power (the twin sacred hearts of this non-sectarian group) Tony did feel comfortable with his own connection to, well, something greater than himself. Standing in front of St. Stephan's felt natural, like rubbing shoulders with an old friend.

Tony pulled back the sleeve of his black leather motorcycle jacket and checked his watch. It was time to take the short walk to his sponsor's new digs. He pushed off from the sidewalk, crossed Ferry Street in front of a low rider blaring Spanish music (nice beat, he thought, maybe I need to hook that into my next song), and turned left into a side street lined with three story stucco houses, each upper floor sprouting a balcony with a bowed-out railing unlike anything he had seen anywhere else in America. He wondered where they got them—was there a special wrought iron monger in the Ironbound who sold only to this area? Where they imported from Iberia?

Many of the houses had decorative ceramic tiles around their entry doors, and some even had tile portraits of saints on their facades, usually drawn in cerulean glaze on sharp white squares. Once again, he wondered where they came from—were they imported from Portugal, or was there some tile maker here in Newark who was known only to the locals? He had to find out, perhaps get one for his estate further west in the Garden State 'burbs. That would be a trip. But he probably should ask Maria, first. Yah, he needed to cut back on that self-centered impulsivity of getting what he wanted without thinking about her needs or about the cost. One more part of the program to keep working. He made a note to mention this to his sponsor as he turned up the short concrete walk to the door of these new digs. One of those ceramic saint portraits was embedded next to the front door.

Over the years and through a number of programs Tony had had several sponsors. Some were barely more dependable than he was, especially in his early years in 12 Step programs when he had not yet learned how to read potential sponsors.

Like the one in AA who actually told him that he thought it was okay to have a social drink once in a while. Crazy, man, just crazy. Tony dumped him but quick. Others were more interested in marching him through the 12 Steps as quickly as they could—Step Sponsors they called themselves. While that was certainly good stuff that had helped him stay clean and sober for over ten years, he never really dug down deeply enough to the core of his addictive personality. And then he wound up in Debtors Anonymous when it was clear that his disease had just done an addiction swap, as they called it, coming out in compulsive spending and debting that was as destructive as any of his other addictions.

Turned out his DA sponsor was the best for him and doubled as Tony's Alcoholics Anonymous sponsor as well. Fred wasn't much older than Tony but his history left behind a craggy face with deep smile lines and steely gray hair close cropped military style. When Fred shared at open meetings, everyone in the room paid close attention because he carried decades of wisdom on recovery. It was kind of intimidating, but on the other hand, this was exactly the kind of challenge that fired up Tony S., as Tony Silvio identified himself at meetings.

Standing on the front step of the Ironbound three story, about to knock on the door, Tony thought back to that first time they sat and talked. Tony had worked up the courage to ask if Fred would be his sponsor. That evening, in the back of a taqueria, Tony laid it all on the table in a long rush of sadness.

"So this is the man behind the Tony Silvio Project. You must think I'm a real mess," Tony said, nervous that this guy would tell him he could not help someone as fucked up as he was.

His new sponsor sat quietly long after Tony finished speaking.

Finally Fred chuckled, "Well, I do think you are insane. Then again, that's why you are in 12 Steps—to come to terms with your insane mind and get healthier. That's why we are all here. We're all insane when it comes to debting and spending. Our minds aren't like normal folks' minds.

"Let's say you have two guys, one who is normal, and one who is a debtor. Both have one hundred dollars in their wallet and a credit card with a thousand-dollar limit. The normal guy thinks to himself, 'Well, I have one hundred dollars to spend.' But the debtor, he thinks, 'I have eleven hundred dollars to spend! And if I play the float right, I can stretch that to over two grand!' And we keep doing it over and over again, thinking that somehow the next time will be different. It's insane."

"But, like, man, I have been through more addictions than they have "A's" for," Tony answered.

Was that a twinge of pride creeping into his voice as well? Could be. Part of being Tony Silvio had been to be more everything than anyone else, whether it was sex, drugs, rock'n'roll, or spending.

Fred just smiled warmly. "Someone once told me that DA is like the PhD curriculum of 12 Step programs. It seems like folks get sobered up in AA or NA when they are younger, but only later figure out that they are not done, that the compulsive behavior has come spurting out again as debting and uncontrolled spending. Look at our meetings—many are recovered alcoholics or clean addicts. AA meetings are our best source of referrals.

"So, nothing you are going to tell me is going to come as a

surprise, and no matter how much you want to shock me, you won't. If at any point you feel like you are not comfortable with working with me, just say so. I'll do the same. We'll just deal with it one step at a time and see where it goes, okay?"

And just like that Tony had taken the plunge and committed to becoming solvent working with this sponsor.

In fact, this is how Tony Silvio the rock musician eventually became a new kind of rock star on the recovery speaker circuit. His celebrity opened doors but, Tony knew, it was his sincerity and humility before the audience at a recovery center or rehab retreat that gave him something to say. People nodded knowingly and when he was done, they applauded.

* * *

Even though Tony cut up all his credit cards three years ago, Maria would remind him he still had that impulsive insanity bubbling inside him.

Worse, he continued to lie, often about trivial things that he did not need to hide. It was still part of the ongoing gabble of craziness that narrated so much of his inner life. Still, with the help of his sponsor, Fred, his manager, Bishop, and the love and faith of Maria, he had hope it would continue to get better.

Tony knocked on Fred's door, three times as he always did, singing in his head, "*Knock three times on the ceiling if you...*" All part of being Tony Silvio. Tony heard the heavy step of his sponsor coming to the door, and he put on his big face grin as the door started to open.

"Yo, Freddie, my man, what a cool joint you moved into!" Tony exclaimed.

Even after years of working together, Fred still would look a bit taken aback at Tony's greeting. Then Fred Kouyoumjian shook his head, smiled that familiar smile around the corners of his lips, and reached out for a big hug.

"C'mon in, Rock Star, let me show you around a bit," he said, stepping back and swinging his right arm into the hallway.

After the tour, the two men settled into Fred's office on the first floor. Tony admired the tiles on the wall behind Fred. What had he called them? *Abuelos*? He had forgotten, his mind after all these years of abuse was not as sharp as he'd like. He rolled the loss around in that same mind like a dull worry and then once he pushed it aside the word came to him. *Azulejos*.

"It's been a while since we last talked," Fred said. "You know you can always call me, even when you are on the road."

"Yah, well, been kinda busy what with the book tour. Also, I'm thinking about getting back into the studio, working on a few new songs."

Fred raised an eyebrow appraisingly. It had been a few years since Tony last wrote new music, and they had discussed Tony's fear that he could only write good stuff when he was on a high of some sort—booze, dope, sex, or spending. Maybe there was a connection between insanity and good rock'n'roll.

"How's the music turning out?"

"You know, I think some of it might be okay," Tony ventured, "Ya' never really know until you get it on the tracks."

Fred looked at Tony, waiting to see if more would come up. Then he said, "Let's start with the Serenity Prayer, okay? Then we can dig into what's going on with you these days."

Even though Tony knew this was coming, part of him felt like he was on the top rise of a huge rollercoaster at the exact moment where it pauses before plunging down the track. He felt an irrational ball of fear knot in his stomach and he had an impulse to get up and leave before it was too late.

But Tony S. had been here before, gone through opening up and trying to be honest, having Fred call him out on his shit. Each time Tony survived, just like being on a huge roller coaster. He could do this.

He took a deep breath and started the prayer. "God," feeling the word vibrate deep in his chest, followed by a long pause, letting his mind sync up with God or calm or whatever it was.

Fred echoed him, and then together, *"Grant me the serenity...."*

10

∾

The Courage to Change the Things I Can

The detective looked across his desk at the talented performer, outsized grey-streaked hair sprouting from the top of his head and disappearing behind the shoulders of a well-worn black leather jacket.

Tony Silvio had a barely suppressed lopsided grin on his face as if planning some mischief or readying some wise-ass comment to throw Fred off balance. It had taken Fred some time to get used to this, to realize that it was more than just armor that Tony wore, a kind of Rock God uniform—it was who Tony Silvio *was*.

It was this crazy mix of ego, energy, and just enough winking self-awareness that allowed Tony Silvio to walk out on stage in huge stadiums and fill the crowd with a sense of vicarious freedom and entitlement.

"So, *yo, yo, yo Mr. Sponsor*, how the hell are *you* doing these days?"

"Hey, I'm doing pretty good, thanks for asking. Had a great call with my own sponsor last night, worked through some stuff about making sure I billed my clients on time. Felt good to get clear on it," Fred said with fondness for Tony *and* the 12 Step program.

Tony picked up on the shift to DA matters. "Man, I am so lucky to have Bishop at my side, y'know? Helps keep all that shit moving for me when I am on the road. One day in Reno, the next day in LA, after that Spokane, jeez, sometimes I wake up in the morning and for ten minutes I can't recall where the hell I am."

"Bishop's a good man. He's working his 12 Step program really well, got strong recovery. I'm glad he is working out well for you. But you know, Tony, only *you* can be responsible for your numbers, even when someone else is putting them together for you."

"Yah, yah, I dig, Fred. Bishop and I have a meeting about 'em every week, Monday morning, Zoom, Skype, whatever, if I am out of town, and I make sure that I own my numbers. And I keep track of everything I spend on this neat app I found for my phone."

Tony started swiping on the screen. He easily got lost in new gadgets, like a young kid sometimes. He leaned over the desk and showed his sponsor the new app that recorded all his daily spending and automatically uploaded it to his accounting system in the cloud. Fred nodded anyway, enjoying Tony's enthusiasm.

Tony caught the look on Fred's face and chuckled.

"I sure do love my toys. But I'll tell you what, Freddy-boy, I am still solvent. This phone was paid for one-hundred percent *in cash*. Came out of my 'toy reserve' that you and I talked about setting up a while back. Every week Bishop peels two hundred bucks into that reserve so that when I really want a new toy, I can buy it. No more whipping out my credit card like my, um, you know...." Tony grinned wickedly, letting the unspoken image dangle in the air. "Back before DA I would just buy anything I wanted without a thought, just whip out that old card until it was smoking from overuse and begging for mercy. If I wanted it, it was mine, and *nothin'* would stop me, kind of the way I approached the ladies, by the way."

"Feels good to be in control, eh?" Fred responded.

Tony nodded sharply, then bounced up and started pacing around the room, looking at pictures on the walls, touching knick knacks on tables, a blur of kinetic energy in motion.

He stopped by a bookshelf and picked up a framed photograph of a young man, perhaps twenty-five years old, and cocked his head at his sponsor. For a moment Fred stared quietly at Tony. Then he said, almost under his voice, "That...is my son. He lives overseas."

Something in his voice stopped Tony from asking anything more. The Tony Silvio Project returned to his chair and sat down letting it swivel, thrusting his legs out in a wide V in front of him like a teenager in health class. Maria called it "manspreading" and he kind of liked the sound of that.

Tony steepled his fingers in front of his lips and took a deep breath, "That's kind of what I am here to talk about today. Kids. I know it's not about debting and spending and DA and all that stuff, but it is about being honest—with myself, with others. And that is a huge issue for me with my program, right?"

"Absolutely," Fred agreed. "We're right back to Step 4 work: *'making a searching and fearless inventory of our character traits'*."

Fred sat back a bit, knowing they had finally gotten to the meat of the meeting. Tony had not told him what was on his mind when he called to ask if he could come by, and Fred knew from experience with this sponsee that he had to let Tony come to the point when he was ready.

Tony swiped to a new screen on his device and shared it with Fred. It was a message announcing, without any real joy, that a baby *boy* had been born.

"It'll take a minute to explain how this kid ties in. You know about how my daughter—my birth-daughter Jessica—found me a while back? After twenty years of not knowing?"

Fred nodded, "Your press agent has done a good job. He really worked that angle."

"Ya, well, it sure sold me a lot more books, got me that great interview and all. But that was not the good thing. The best thing was simply looking in my daughter's eyes, man, and seeing some of me reflected back in her. *And then* seeing more of her than me, and enjoying that as well. I never realized how...primordial it would feel to be with your own kid." He rolled the word "primordial" around. Liked the sound of that one.

Fred wondered if it would wind up in his next song.

"You know what I mean, I mean, you have your own son, so you get it," Tony ventured, trying to make an emotional connection with his sponsor. Fred just looked at Tony with no reaction, which Tony took as license to continue.

"Anyhow, because everyone knows about my story, I guess I

have become kind of like a beacon for dads reuniting with their lost kids. I can't tell you how many fans have sent me tweets and emails telling me about their reunions, or how they wanted to find their own kid they abandoned years before. My publicist takes care of them, sends them information on searching, a photo I have signed with a special message for dads, but I still read a lot of the stuff that comes in.

"Then the other day one of my neighbors comes a-knockin' on my door" (he couldn't help the sing-song voice) "and says he had a special favor to ask of me. Nice guy, former business executive of something in his polo shirt and khakis, you could tell he was not all that comfortable speaking to a rock'n'roller. The favor was that a son of a friend of his had gotten a girl knocked up and the kid was not taking responsibility for it. This neighbor, Clay, he asked if I would talk to the boy, see if I could help him understand what was what as a, you know, birth-father who had just been found."

At the mention of Clay, Fred cocked his head and looked at Tony for a moment. "This Clay. Is he about sixty-five years old, tall, full head of white hair, business executive you said?"

Tony stopped fidgeting and stared in slight amazement at his sponsor. He was used to Fred saying things that turned his head inside out, but that was usually something about not debting or some drop of wisdom from AA-speak. But how the heck did Fred in the Ironbound know Clay from way out in the suburbs? Tony guessed that Fred had come across Clay during some special investigation that his corporation had contracted out.

"Uh, yeah, that sure sounds like the man. Do you know him?"

Fred hesitated for a moment, wrestling with his commitment to anonymity for both his 12 Step programs and his private investigation business. Then Tony watched his sponsor nod as if completing an argument with himself and sit forward, his elbows propped on the red desk blotter before him.

"Tony, one of the things I specialize in for my private practice is helping adoptees find their birth-families. More recently I help donor-conceived people and their intentional parents track down genetic relatives from back in the 'anonymous donor' days."

Tony nodded, "Go on, Freddo."

"Lately, as part of this, I have become involved with a group of birth-fathers, and one of them is Clay. I guess it is okay to 'out' him because I know he is very public about his situation himself. The fact that he came to you is not an accident—he has been attending meetings of an adoption circle that is a program for adult adoptees, donor-conceived people, and parents. Clay's been thinking and talking about this stuff deeply. If he sought you out, it was with a reason."

He knew Fred was getting at more than the deposition or the court case. Uncharacteristically, Tony sat still and did not fidget for a while. He watched a shaft of sunlight coming in through the sheer drape covering a window, then slowly looked at Fred's bookcase again, not noticing the titles.

"I guess now is the time I'm supposed to say that this is my Higher Power giving me a chance to do something, right," Tony said with more than a dose of sarcasm.

Even after going through a number of spiritual programs he still struggled with the idea that God, or his Higher Power, or whatever, would actually give a damn about an ex-druggie old pop singer. *Why would he come to me with this? What do I have to offer? I mean, I never even knew I had a daughter, let alone raised a kid.* These were ideas he and Fred worked on together each time Tony phoned since getting that first call from Jessica.

Tony added, "Actually, it wasn't the first time Clay cornered me at one of the country clubs in town. He asked me to testify as a witness, you know, from my experience as a birth-father. I met with this attorney who put together a pool of birth-fathers. The name pops: The Birth-Fathers' Club. They're getting together to restore access to original birth certificates for adult adoptees."

"I'm familiar with the Birth-Father's Club. Clay and I talked. Did you help them?"

"Just last week. At Ted Landtsman's on Park Avenue. He's quarterbacking it. I don't figure how I added much. They've already got birth-fathers that have been following this for years. That actually tried to search for their kid, like Clay is. I guess they just needed my brand to sell their paperwork. Know what I mean?"

Tony watched Fred nod and felt more centered before going on. "But this new request. I dunno – Clay has kids. They're all, like, in the same wealthy enclave, same schools. I just don't know what I'm supposed to say to this kid. I know as much about fatherhood as the kid does. I blew Maria's chance so it seems, to have a baby, and blew my chance to support Jessica growing up."

"You always have trouble accepting that God does not make junk," Fred said quietly. "Instead of asking, 'why me?', how about flipping the script and saying, 'why not me?' Doing estimable action gives us self-esteem, as it says in the Big Book."

"But what if I fuck it up, Fred?" Tony said with real anguish in his voice. "What if I tell the kid to do the wrong thing? How the hell am I supposed to know what is good for him, for his kid, for the girl? Should I tell him to try to keep the kid himself? *Should I encourage him to sign off on the adoption?* Maybe he would be the lousiest parent ever and I talk him into keeping a kid who gets raised in hell?"

The world-weary detective's eyes crinkled and softened. This was familiar territory for them.

"You don't have to have an answer when you walk in the door, Tony, you know that. Rely on your Higher Power, listen to your gut, ask God for the words. Meditate on it, say the Serenity Prayer, and see where it all goes. Actually, let's sit with it for a few minutes right now."

Tony envisioned meeting with the boy, felt his breathing pick up. Tony leapt to his feet jerkily and started pacing around the room again. "I dunno, man, I don't think I can do this. Why did Clay ask me? Maybe if I ignore him he'll go away."

"Tony, you are feeling fear. Go back to the basics of the program. You know what "fear" stands for, right?"

"*Fuck* Everything And *Run*!" It felt good to swear, and Tony put a lot of emotion into the first word.

Fred chuckled patiently. "Right, but it also means 'face everything and recover.' The way to deal with fear is action, not retreat. Meaningful action. Throw it out there and see what comes up. You don't have to control everything or have every answer. Trust in your Higher Power, listen to your Higher Power in the moment, and I am sure you will do the right thing when the time comes. It is important for your recovery to get outside of yourself and provide strength for this boy, to provide service. See it as an opportunity, not a burden. Part of your Step 12 work is to leave the world a better place than you found it," Fred said before flicking a glance at the wall clock.

"Now, you need to wrap up and get on to making some money today, Fred, my man. Serenity Prayer?"

Fred nodded slightly and they said the prayer slowly before saying their good-byes.

Tony always felt clearer and somewhat relieved after talking with Fred, but as he walked down the Ironbound pavement toward where he parked his bike, he still felt uncertain about how the talk would go with the kid Dan.

But at least he was now unshakably certain that he was going to meet with Dan.

11

Backstage

Tony suggested that the meeting with Dan take place at an upcoming Tony Silvio concert, and Clay acted as chauffer, accompanying Dan to the green room just off-stage at the Prudential Center. Bishop made sure they were set up on the naugahyde couches in one of the nicer dressing rooms where they could listen to the soundchecks while they waited for Tony Silvio.

Tony stood quietly in the hallway for a few moments, riffing on some ideas. He knew that Fred would want him to say the Seventh Step prayer at this point to center his energy and focus on the task at hand. How did it go? Something like "I stand ready to carry your message to others. Help me be who you want me to be." Tony never could remember that stuff, was always grudgingly impressed with the folks at meeting who could roll out those AA sayings with no effort. But the general thought of simply doing what needed to be done was comforting to him and his breathing slowed a bit as he got the hunch that he would know the right words to say.

Another line popped into his head, that when the teacher was ready, the student would appear. Was that AA or was that the karate movie? It was such a drag when the wires in his brain crossed. So fucking old before his time. Enough philosophizing.

Tony remembered also that when he was Dan's age no one could tell him anything, especially some old dude. And no matter what age the messenger, Dan might not be ready to hear *this* message. Tony Silvio would give it his best shot, he decided, as he flexed his fingers and rolled up and down on his toes to work out some tension in his legs. Tony took a deep breath, put on his best Tony Silvio smile, and bounded through the door like the Rock Star he was.

When Tony came through the doorway the energy was infectious even for a normally contemptuous teenager. This was Tony Silvio after all, up close, back stage. The kid looked up at him and greeted him with a barely contained light of recognition, just a glimmer of eagerness in his eyes.

The kid stood up and Tony wrapped him in a big hug. Tony had not planned to do this, but it just seemed right at the moment, and Tony was all about going with the moment, so long as it no longer involved booze, drugs or money shenanigans. The impulsive side of him still ruled otherwise, whether he was writing songs or shopping for food.

Clay almost laughed out loud at the look on Dan's face, smooshed up against the black leather jacket of the much taller and wiry stage performer. One thing for certain, the Tony Silvio Project definitely cracked through the kid's diffident disdain in a hurry. Clay idly wondered if he could have ever used that hug opening in a business meeting. It was almost as amusing as watching Dan stumble a bit as Tony Silvio wrapped an arm over his shoulders and steered him towards the banquet table.

Tony plunged in, "Man, congratulations on your son. I heard you became a dad. Have something to eat, dude, you gotta be hungry."

Dan nodded uncertainly, either at the thought of being a father or the strangeness of being fed by Tony Silvio. The kid was looking stunned but slowly coming to accept the fact that this was really happening to him. Meanwhile Tony Silvio filled the air with electricity and patter, keeping the whole show moving.

"You gotta try this caviar, man. I have it imported from Latvia. Organic shad. What, you never tried caviar?"

Dan was looking almost as green as the walls at the sight of it.

"Ok, well, then the salsa, try the salsa. From Paul Newman's special reserve batch," Tony winked at Clay over Dan's shoulder, having a bit of fun with the kid now.

Dan was starting to recover and began looking around the room as if something was missing. Tony immediately tripped to what the kid was thinking.

"Nah, man, no dope, no booze. I don't do that shit anymore, and neither does my band. I'm like Keith, you know, like they had to give me transfusions to get all the crap outta my system before I went into rehab."

"Keith? You mean Keith Richards. Isn't he, like, eighty?"

The kid flopped back in the slung bucket seat he had been waiting in for Tony.

Tony didn't want to lose him, "Ever listen to his stuff?"

This kid must not be a fan—hadn't even brought up Tony's first hit "*Big Hair Love*", the band's anthem "*Shoot the Alarm*" or the acoustic version of "*Wedding Vow Hearts*". Tony had never learned how to appreciate people who weren't fans or groupies. It seemed so much work. Something he would have to bring up with Fred one of these days, if Fred did not trip to it first.

The kid bit into a fat burrito, the laminated plate balanced precariously on his knees. "Yeah, I heard it sampled." Then the kid seemed to remember himself, "I downloaded '*Shoot the Alarm*', paid for it on a legit fileshare site. Sounds like you had the whole stadium joining in."

Tony smiled. Now they were talking.

"And my buddy, Josh, he saw you guys down at Virginia Beach last year, with his old man."

"That was a good night. Really rocked out," Tony smiled. And, he told himself, it was a good night because he could remember it. He could not say that about many of his concerts from decades gone by.

"Yeah, that's what Josh said! I can't believe you're really here, man. Like, I'm really talking to you. And, hey, I know that my folks and her folks have been talking and that Clay knows too. Like you had a kid who just found you and we could talk about it—hey, I bet you had a lot of kids on the road."

Tony winced at the offhand way Dan said this. Sure, it came along with the iconography of the Tony Silvio Project, but it was no longer funny. Tony was growing up, finally, and realizing that real people got hurt in this life, that it was not a myth.

"Just the one," he said. Then he looked intensely into Dan's eyes and tried to put real seriousness into it, "her name is Jessica."

There was an awkward pause as Tony remembered the fight with Maria when he first told her about his daughter. The *fact* that it still *bothered* him really bothered him, and he knew he had a lot of work to do with this one, a lot of amends to make, but he got back on to the matter at hand, "Dan-o, this is the part where you're supposed to pull out your wallet and show me pics of the little man."

"'Little man?' You mean Anna's kid?" Dan looked surprised to have been asked so suddenly, and then looked away at the table of food to his right.

"Dan," Tony said quietly, waiting.

The kid leaned forward without getting up, swiped his hand behind his jacket and slid his phone out of his back pocket. Tony was only guessing but it turned out he had called it right: Dan did indeed have pictures but on his phone not in a wallet—of course. Dan's lowered head was backlit by the late morning sun coming in through the wide picture window. Black hair at his nape spiked out like a huskie's just above a narrow knotted leather lace. When the kid leaned back Tony saw it looped through a hole in the center of a circle of purple jade.

"Jade. Chinese. For good luck, right? I have a tat with the same characters."

"Nah, this one isn't Chinese. There's no characters," said Dan matter-of-factly, not really calling Tony out on the white lie, "It's Guatemalan. They have jade, too, down there."

Dan held the amulet for a moment, then looked up at Tony before continuing, subdued, "We. We Guatemalans have it, too. My parents brought it back when they brought me back. Gave it to me for my eighteenth birthday," he shrugged and then to add some distance, "Really wanted a car."

He considered this, that the boy himself was adopted and all the whorl of emotions that might imply. Tony Silvio took a deep breath before launching in with, "Look, I heard something about the relinquishment conversation between you and your son's mother. That's actually why they asked me to speak to you."

The kid looked up from underneath the fringe over his eyes. "Yah, I know." Then he glowered at a spot on the floor between his sneakers, like he was about to be forced to listen to another adult lecture him.

Tony continued, "I wasn't really *with* her birth-mother, you know. We just hooked up at a party, I barely even remember what she looked like. She could have been one of any number of groupies I got it on with back in the day. Then, I get a phone call out of the blue—twenty-one years later—and it's someone named Jessica. My daughter.

"Part of me wonders if it was not a blessing in disguise that her birth-mother never told her about me. I wasn't a good candidate for father of the year, I was so wasted and blitzed those years. I really wonder if I woulda been in a condition to raise her even if I'd known."

Tony did his best not to sound preachy, speaking just above a whisper, "I lost years. I lost brain cells. Yeah, but that's not what I'm here to say and you're not ready to listen."

Dan sighed and shifted around in the seat of his chair.

Tony stared hard at the boy in front of him., "They're about to fuck you over so bad you can't even imagine."

Dan's face went deadpan but the change was too quick.

Good, Tony thought. That pulled him up short.

"What are you talking about?" Dan asked in a careful voice.

"Signing the TPR, man. They want you to give away your own flesh and blood because it is easy for all of them, and you haven't even realized what that is going to mean to you."

Dan curled his lip and growled, "No one's doing anything to me. You can't make me raise that kid. She's the one who didn't use birth control. She told me she was safe, that we didn't need no jimmy cap, but the bitch lied. It's not my fault we're all fucked up like this now."

Tony Silvio put his big paws on his knees like he was getting ready to stand up.

Dan's face fell.

Tony eased back into the chair.

"It's not about that girl, or what you think of her. I don't know her. I wasn't even with the mother of my child. Then I meet my kid and it's like a clap of thunder. *My* kid. Do you *get* what I am sayin' here? This is not about that girl. It is about you and your own son and what you plan to do about him."

"Are you one of those anti-adoption people my parents and their infertility friends used to complain about?" Dan looked uncomfortable as soon as he said it and his gaze slid toward the door. The last people he wanted to be allied with were his parents but he needed to say something. He hadn't expected Tony Silvio to be this intense.

Tony continued unflappable, "I never thought about adoption, pro or con."

It was true he hadn't even known he'd gotten Cyrena pregnant. Even if she had told him he was pretty certain that the Tony Silvio Project of that time would have let her make any decision she wanted, short of offering the child to him to raise. He was glad that he had finally started to grow up, even this late in his life.

"I'm not even talking about whether it is right for your kid to be adopted or not. I'm talking about your son."

"Huh?"

"TPR, man. I'm talking about termination of parental rights, *termination of your rights as a father,*" Tony paused to look away. He wanted the kid to have some grasp of what he would be losing or taking on, whatever he chose. Tony did the centered breathing thing before continuing, "Shit, show me those pics."

12

In the Green Room

It was then that Tony noticed Dan's shaking hands holding the phone. Part of Tony wondered if the kid had skipped his morning high or beer or whichever Breakfast of Champions he sucked down each day. But another part recognized that the kid was feeling real emotions talking about his child, even if perhaps he could not identify or understand them fully.

The first three photos were some selfies. The girl had long blonde hair, blue eyes and a narrow aquiline face, all seen at a slightly weird angle as she held the phone in one hand, the baby crooked in her other arm.

Dan said, "She's from Poland."

"Adopted, too?"

The young father nodded.

Tony sucked in his breath.

There were three more pictures, family shots. The girl was beaming, proud for the moment. Dan was leaning in over her as she held their baby. The baby was swaddled in the hospital's thin flannel bunting. A tiny rose brown face peeked out, flashing a rich dark tuft of hair.

"Got your hair," Tony said and waited the flick of a second before the boy's chest seemed to fill out.

"Yup. Skin's kinda half and half."

"Whose ears?"

"Oh, hers. You can't tell because her hair's down in front but definitely hers," the young man said, warming to the conversation. The mother was a pretty girl. Dan must have or still did like her, Tony Silvio guessed. To the extent that this stoner could give any shit at all about someone else.

He looked at the hands holding the photos. They weren't shaking anymore. Maybe he'd been wrong about that morning high.

"Whose hands and feet? I can't tell with your kid all wrapped up like that."

Now Dan actually laughed, "Mine." There was nothing really funny, nothing unusual about Dan's digits as far as Tony could tell. The laughter was from surprise.

Tony realized something else, "Hey if you're adopted, you've never seen anyone like you before. Man, this is your very first blood relative, the first time you've ever met DNA family, huh?"

Tony might as well have socked Dan in the eye. The kid looked punch drunk.

"Damn, see, this is what I was trying to tell you," Tony slapped his thigh, "*You already know it.* They're trying to get you to surrender your first born. You think about maybe you'd be cheating yourself." Then Tony leaned forward, "Are they telling you what you owe him? That you can't handle it? That the kid's better off without you? Maybe you're even telling yourself a man's gotta look out for himself. Am I right?"

Dan nodded, not sure where this was going, but trying not to act fazed by someone seeing into him faster than he could see into himself. Tony Silvio of all people.

For his part, Tony had surprised himself with his own fervor. When Tony walked into the room he truly had no idea what he was going to say to the boy. But the more he talked to Dan, and the more he projected his own feelings about Jessica onto the situation, the more convinced he became that the right path for Dan, for most birth-fathers in fact, was to stay involved in the lives of their children somehow. Tony wondered if he needed to dial it back, put some other options on the table for Dan, perhaps suggest that he simply take some time before making up his mind. Then before he realized it he was back on his soapbox.

"It's what you owe yourself. Don't let them cheat *you*. This is your kid. I guarantee they'll find a couple with more money, not adopted, you name it. They may even slip you some cash, say it's to help you move on with your life. You won't. None of you will. That couple will love the baby, sure, he'll take their name. Maybe never want to search for you because you were just his deadbeat old man—don't let them sell you on 'that's healthy'."

Now Dan looked stone cold sober.

"I could tell you that you owe it to your kid with your digits and your hair, but..." Tony let his words drift as he noted to himself that even after his rant Dan's eyes lit up when Tony reminded the kid what the baby boy shared with him.

Tony was watching Dan fighting it back. He might bolt so Tony finally brought it down a notch but continued. "It's what you owe yourself. You don't have to just go along with whatever decision other people make for you and your kid. Get some more information, take the time to think things through. Just take it one day at a time."

He surprised himself with that last one. It was a line he first heard in NA. You commit to staying clean one day at a time. This kid wasn't going to college. Maybe community a few years from now. But he needed a job or jobs. He needed to wake up every morning, get dressed, get out and then set his alarm every night. Offering him a vision of his very own blood relative might be enough incentive.

But Lord knows the world was full of adoption attorneys waiting for Dan to stumble and catch his baby if he fell. Like dealers waiting for you to fall off the wagon.

Tony kept going with the metaphors. He was only improvising but doing it well.

"Like I lost years with booze. I lost years with my only effing, excuse me, I lost out on raising my only daughter. When we're together, we're tight. I wish I'd been there for her. God I wish I had. I can get down on my knees and thank the true man who raised her, him and his wife."

"You mean her adoptive parents?"

"Yes," Tony replied, "This kid'll give you a reason to live. You will eff-ing WANT to get up out of bed because you'll want your son to have his own soccer ball. You'll WANT to get your act together because you'll want him to be proud of you, proud of where he came from even if you don't know the hell why your own old man in Guatemala let you be given away. You'll want to stand on your own two feet, more than just picking fights with your—" Tony paused, thinking of using the old sobriety line that 'battles aren't boundaries' but decided it would be over Dan's head at this age. He'd try something else, "You'll want your Dad to be proud of you, like he always used to be. Even if he says it now neither of you believe it anymore. You'll want to tell that lawyer to go stick it up his own ass but to stay the hell away from you and your kid. If they haven't already, they'll start showing you binders of couples advertising for your baby. You don't need the 'loving, middle-class couple with a golden retriever'. You *can* do this if you want to."

"B-but, her parents were talking about maybe an open adoption. You know, we come to the birthday party every year. Maybe even if the parents are around we're allowed to see him once a month—" Dan said robotically.

"You sound like my GPS. What does your girl want?"

"She wants to give the kid up for adoption, says it's the best chance our son will have for a normal life."

"They told you all that stuff about what they'll do once they've got the goods, the baby? Sounds like a record deal I once had when I was starting out, my boy. I call it taking it up the rear and I mean—"

"Hey! You—."

"The word's *enforcement*, baby. You got friends whose parents are divorced?"

"Yeah. What does that have to do with—?"

"What do their folks complain about when it comes to family court?

"The moms complain about the dads not paying enough. Or paying late, whatever, not abiding by the child support agreement. The dads complain about the moms moving away so they can't see their kid."

"Bingo. *Enforcement*. Family court can give you a pretty piece of paper setting visitation in black and white—but if mom takes the kids five states away the kids hardly see dad: there's no enforcement. Open adoption is no better than that. Think about it."

"You mean if they move or don't want us to visit?"

"Yeah. Your kid is gone baby gone," Tony was surprising himself: he wanted to get through to this new parent, "Next up, what if they decide you're a bad influence? Say, you give the old man the creeps because of your tats, or, what if mom is too fragile to handle the stress of her kid having an extra set of parents. What if? Gone baby gone. You keep your son, you get a job, no one can touch you or your son. He's your number one family now."

Tony paused and just looked at this kid. This would have been the moment to offer him a spot on the crew. The kid would take it, he knew.

Tony instead reached into his wallet to hand him a card. He wanted to see if the kid would make some effort first: call Tony up, ask for a job.

"Listen, us old NAs do this, we 'sponsor' the newbies. We've already walked the walk, and don't just spew the talk. You ain't lost your kid yet."

It was clear Dan wasn't happy with the idea of surrendering his baby. He didn't have what they called it, a vision plan, to replace it with. The new father looked down at Tony's card, even paused to type it into his phone before putting it away. He kept his head bowed for a moment. Then Bishop leaned his shiny head into the room and told him they had to get going, the concert was going to be starting soon.

"Bishop, give us three."

Bishop nodded and ducked his head back out.

Tony stood up and cuffed Dan gently on the shoulder, "You've got my card. Let's talk again. Oh, and I am trusting you here—that's my personal cell phone number, so don't be giving it out to anyone, okay?"

The kid numbly nodded in agreement, still not completely processing the situation. "They told me I have to decide within seven days. Two more days left."

"Or else what? You're the dad. As long as you agree to take the baby and don't screw up, they can't tell you nothing. Two days! You're the *dad*. Tell them your people will call their people."

Tony was pleased when he heard Dan laugh. The boy wasn't used to being the one who held the cards.

"You're still living with your folks, right?"

"Yeah."

"You pay them rent?"

"Nah."

"And I bet you never thank them for it," he said more to himself than Dan. Then he focused back on the kid, "When you get on your feet, give them some bills, you'll feel like a man. Any jobs?"

"One at Game-a-teria. Only seventeen hours a week."

"Ask for more and keep looking. If they won't give you more you can tell them to kiss your ass—after you find a full-time gig. Even if they do give you more, keep looking. They pay shit, don't they?"

"Yeah, minimum wage."

"No benies, right?"

The kid looked confused.

"Benefits. Health insurance to save you money when you take your kid to the doctor in four weeks." Tony knew that tidbit from when one of his bandmates became a father, "you're okay for now because your folks can cover you until you're twenty-six. But between you and me, the sooner you get out from under them the better you'll feel. Don't cut them out. Your old man can still teach you a thing or two because he's seen more than you, if you know what I mean. Most people are cool, but the more *family* you have the better for your kid. You gotta think smarter now, look out for *him*."

"I've never babysat. I've never even given a baby a bottle."

"She breastfeeding?"

"Yeah, she is."

"Scratch that off the list then, for now. How old were you when they brought you home from Guatemala?"

"I dunno. Still a baby."

"Then your folks can show you what to do."

"God, I—"

"It doesn't mean you have to do it exactly their way. Just remember, you've got to start thinking smarter. Watch some of their moves, maybe even do it the same for a while 'til you get the hang of it."

Bishop was on the other side of the door. Both of them felt him getting ready to knock.

"One day at a time. Call me in the morning. Hell, call me tonight. I'm clean so I pick up now."

Tony opened the door where Bishop stood with Tony's jacket and scarves. He turned back to look deeply at Clay, still sitting quietly in the corner of the green room, and wondered if perhaps he had gone too far, way too far.

Tony could only hope he had paid it forward with this kid.

* * *

The next morning around eleven Tony Silvio awoke to golden sunlight streaming onto his bedcovers. The concert the night before had run to three rousing encores, capped with a cover of the Stones' *"You Can't Always Get What You Want"* that Tony knew was going to be a bootleg prize circulating for years. Tony and the band just slayed it—the song had special meaning for him ever since that day he met Jessica in the studio, and it reverberated in his performances.

He rolled over onto the soft flat plain on the bed where Maria had not been the night before. It was now a week since he'd even heard her voice on the phone. He breathed in Maria's scent lingering on her pillow—jasmine and lavender and something spicy he could not place but which always reminded him of her soft skin.

Dan.

Tony's mind went back to the talk with Dan just before showtime. Tony surprised himself at how heated he got, telling Dan to try to keep his kid, or at least keep a strong relationship with his son. Obviously Tony was channeling his own sorrow and loss over not having known Jessica until she was a grown woman.

Tony lay in bed a long time letting his mind wander over meadows and playgrounds and vacations filled with a baby Jessica growing into a teenager and then a young woman, scenes he never had the chance to have. A deep and hollow sense of not even knowing what he lost settled in the pit of his stomach.

Tony sat up and grabbed his cell phone sitting on the glass-topped nightstand next to the bed. He had Jessica's number on speed dial.

She picked up after two rings.

"Hey, Jess, it's Tony."

"I saw that on caller ID."

"So, how're ya doing?"

She hesitated a moment before answering, still not used to hearing from Tony like he had been around her all her life. For Jessica, it took some getting used to. He wasn't her dad, but he was her father, and she was still figuring out how they could best relate.

"I'm doing great, thanks. Really busy at work, but really liking what I am doing."

Tony nodded to himself, feeling like a dad at some level: happy to hear she was happy. Then he took a deep breath, "Jess, look, I didn't call just to check in. I been thinking about us, you know, how you found me and all, and how grateful I am that you did."

"Me too," she added.

He smiled, "Yah, well, you know me. I am so full of myself, always talking about me and how happy I am, or how I am feeling about things. But I realized that I never really asked you how you felt about it all."

Jessica hesitated again. "'About it all'?"

"Yah, um, I mean, you seem so up and positive all the time about this, uh, strange situation we are in. I mean, like, well, all those years you were growing up and you knew you had a birth-father out there but not *who* he was. Not there for you. How come you are not bitter or angry at the whole thing? I mean, I gotta wonder, if it were me, I think I would be kind of pissed off at my birth-father, my birth-mom, everyone who stuck me in this situation, you know? And yet you seem so chill about it."

Jessica chuckled warmly into the phone and said, "Well, I'm not you. I guess there were times when I did wonder who you were and where you were, but I figured out pretty early on that wondering and daydreaming would not bring you out of the shadows. Mom and Dad, my adoptive parents, were great. I guess at some level deep inside I always knew that I would find you when the time was right and I let it go at that."

Tony lay back into his bespoke memory foam pillows. His daughter sounded a whole lot more mature than he was. "So, you're not angry at me or bitter about it?"

"Nope."

"Well, that's cool. I admire you a lot, Jess, I really do. You are one special lady."

"Why, thank you kind sir. You're being so, um, formal!" Jessica said.

"Ok, well, I'll let you go now, talk to you soon."

"Ok, bye, and thanks for calling. Oh, and Tony, don't worry, I am not angry, really, I mean it."

"Got it, thanks."

Tony stared at the phone for a minute, then placed it back on the night table. It made a slight clink that echoed in the now silent room.

13

✺

Walk This Way

A few days after the concert, Tony Silvio was sitting, parked outside the steps of the judicial complex in the stretch Humvee the attorney Ted Landtsman arranged.

Tony decided to check in with his sponsor Fred to let him know about the visit with Dan. He asked Bishop for some privacy so he could call Fred himself.

Tony noticed that ever since they'd come back from the visit to the law firm, Bishop the Glove had been worrying that they might be squandering the Tony Silvio Project glam here on too small a turnout. Now Tony smiled as he watched Bishop outside the car wading through a sea of relinquishees—people who had been relinquished by one or both sides of their DNA families into fostercare and adoptions—and their allies. A few black-clad radicalized donor-conceived picketers from Bastard Battalion were chanting in a clutch. To one side were the adoptive parents of E.A.R.—Ethical Adoption Referendum. They had all shown up for his testimony. No worries now. Tony could see Bishop was thriving in the throng gathering at the top of the courthouse stairs. The Glove looked to be having some fun rapping with folks from both sides. Probably trying to talk them into buying copies of *Birth of the True*, Tony mused.

Tony had his sponsor on speed dial. Fred picked up right away and asked, "You get any sense which way this kid Dan's gonna break?"

"I didn't get the feeling he knew himself. Nah, but he's got my card. Clay's in touch with his folks. Oh, yeah, and *Maria's still not in touch with me*. I can't reach her in *effin'* Madrid."

"That sucks. She may need time. After you and she not having a child, and then another affair coming to light, and you having a child with another woman—"

"—Got it, got it," Tony snarled irascibly, suddenly wanting to move the conversation to something else.

Fred was not having it. "It must have pushed a lot of buttons and you just can't 'own' her reaction. It's an opportunity to step outside the ego box and put yourself in her shoes. Then put it down. You did what you needed to do: acknowledge your daughter and tell Maria yourself instead of letting her find out from some journalist."

Tony capitulated and agreed, "Yeah, I did that to her in the past. I've changed," and he was indeed glad not to be that person who let the bodies fall where they may. Tony had courted enough chaos in his life, strewn more than his share of damage in the lives of those closest to him. It actually felt good to not be the master of chaos anymore—most of the time.

He had another thought. He decided to share with Fred now what he wouldn't with Bishop or the band because he didn't want to be a buzzkill, not yet anyway.

"Maria may finally be done with me, Fred."

His sponsor was quiet for a long moment. Tony heard him take a deep breath on the other end of the line. "She might be. You can't 'own that' either. Just take it one day at a time. So, you know the slogan: what's the next RIGHT thing you can do?"

The noise was growing around Tony outside the car, he let it distract him. He picked up on the energy, loved it. They were here partly because of him afterall. The number of people outside must have doubled but no one noticed him yet through the heavily shaded windows of the stretch Humvee. He focused back on Fred.

"You mean Steps 8 and 9?"

"Yes," and then his sponsor began to recite the familiar words of this part of the 12 Steps program, "'*make a list of people you have harmed and become willing to make amends to them all; make direct amends to such people wherever possible except when to do so would injure them or others*'. So testifying as part of The Birth-Fathers' Club is one way of getting right with your better self. You and I never had to fight to know our roots, Tony. Adoptees and donor-conceived people like Jessica do have a right to know theirs, too, no matter what the adoption and ART industries think that will do to their profits."

"That's what it's about. The so-called counsellors working on commission for a cut of the baby. I never asked for 'privacy' from my own kid and no one ever promised it. And I am damned grateful she found me," Tony said.

He watched through the darkened glass as Ted walked toward him. Some of the activists holding signs realized now it was the Tony Silvio Project parked at the curb. Show time. He'd wrap up with Fred.

"Okay, I'm ready. I'm going up there. Thanks, Fred."

"Tony, call me whenever. Let me know how it goes." Before the call ended Fred could hear the crowd grow louder as Tony opened the car door. They must have recognized Tony Silvio.

Must be a happy guy, Fred thought knowing Tony well.

Tony reviewed Ted's strategy in his mind. Put Tony up there for this trial against the two plaintiffs the industry found. Their case would be tried here in Manhattan. Clay would be called too. For Tony this appearance would be a chance to try out his chops in front of a courtroom. His body thrummed with the nervous yet confident adrenaline rush he felt before stepping out on stage. He was excited to be embarking on a new phase of his public career, half of him wondering if he would choke up facing the judge and lawyers from the industry, the other half thinking that if he could work a crowd of fifty-thou then he could surely hold this room. Tony loved taking risks, loved walking out on a tightrope without a net. It felt even better doing it sober and for something bigger than himself.

* * *

Testimony took most of the morning. After the hearing was adjourned the judge asked Ted and the industries' attorney-of-record to stay behind for procedural consultation in chambers.

Everyone else on the team streamed out with activists and supporters into the high-ceilinged ground floor lobby. They took up one side of the building.

Ted finally came out through the double doors of the hearing room and caught Tony Silvio's eye. You couldn't miss the tall rock'n'roller, sitting with his bio daughter Jessica on one of the carved wooden benches worn shiny by a century of people sitting and waiting for trials to begin or end.

Tony Silvio wore a midnight jacket and tie over leather pants. When Tony noticed Ted, he gave Jessica's arm a squeeze before pushing himself up to stride over to the middle of the hall. With each step, a dozen oxidized chains swayed in dark rainbows from Tony's belt loops.

The members of the crowd moved apart for the shade-wearing Tony Silvio Project. Ted loved these moments as much as Tony did.

Just as Ted held out his arm to shake hands, Tony made a fist and Ted awkwardly changed formation to bump it. Tony covered a smirk at the lawyer's stiff discomfort. Instead, Tony clapped him on the back, saying, "We're gonna win? Ah, the sweet taste of victory!"

"Yes, my closing statement persuaded the judge, I think. He was nodding slightly in agreement, which is always a good sign," Ted said and then quickly added, "And he was blown away by you, man! They were expecting Screamin' Jay Hawkins but you came off thoughtful, restrained, and damned sincere. You hit it out of the park, Tony, we can't thank you enough. But," Ted said holding up a finger, "It's a landmark case, quite frankly. Our adversaries have a strong lobby and lots of money behind them. They'll have to appeal, at least to save face. The judge knows that so he'll likely as not issue a stay—preventing the adoptee birthright bill from going into effect—until it's worked its way through the system. Adoptees won't have equal access to their original birth certificates and adoption records just yet. Same for donor-conceived people who are still barred from knowing who their anonymous donor is. In other words, until the plaintiffs have a chance to file that appeal."

"And then the records are opened?" Tony asked expectantly. The group behind and to each side of him was listening.

Ted shook his head, "The Appellate court may extend the stay until they've had a chance to render a decision."

Tony cocked his head and pretended to lose interest but he asked, "How long will that take?"

"Don't know, I'll do my best to keep them from delaying it but it's really up to the judge," Ted answered.

"Do I need to be here for that?" Tony said and it was clear the question was rhetorical.

Ted decided to let Tony's question hang for a moment because despite all the work and historic importance, Ted's star Rock God birth-father reminded him of a kid whining from the back seat, "Are we there yet? Are we there yet?"

Ted reached out a hand to hold on to Tony Silvio's sleeve, "I'll let your publicist know that your testimony will have been key in restoring the rights of Jessica and other adoptees in the state." Then he turned his attention to the rest of the packed hall, "Thank you everyone. I know the court was impressed by the level of support you showed and the numbers of us that turned up. Thank you."

Ted looked for Clay's face in the crowd, then added, "When we've got their decision I'll let The Birth-Fathers' Club know and you can pass it along to any other lists or activist accounts."

Hearing this, it dawned on Tony that this wasn't happening within a nice neat hour like some legal drama. This was how the hamster wheel of justice kept turning.

The blonde PR woman cleared her throat and took over in

a voice that was a trace too loud, "We'll prepare the message for you but I'll be communicating directly with the media. If they call you, refer them to me. Single point of contact."

Tony was amused at her striving but decided to let it go. The larger group started breaking up and Ted turned to him, "My car's here. I've got some new scotch we—and whoever you want to bring—can open back at my office!—oh, and seven flavors of seltzer and sparkling water!"

The group broke out in good natured laughter.

"I'll call ahead to make sure they know you all are coming." Ted's hand swept over the crowd, encompassing the birth-fathers, their families who had come along, and Tony's usual retinue of assistants and band mates.

Then Tony Silvio let them figure out the transportation while he turned back to say good-bye to Jessica. "You're still sitting there?"

"I don't think I'll be coming. I still have a long ride home. My folks are waiting..." and Jessica let the sentence fade. Then she perked up, "Call me a limo?"

Neither of his girl's adoptive parents were here. He wondered how they were with this reunion. He'd never stopped to think about them much. The world seemed to get a little more spacious when he thought of that other angle on the reunion. Yeah, must be a whole lot of stuff for them too. Different from him, but still a whole lot of stuff.

* * *

Ensconced in a three-room office suite, one of Tony's group

found the remote for the widescreen. Ted usually only used it to preview security footage from CCTV or videotaped testimony and was about to stop him but decided it added to the atmosphere and let the hanger-on turn to the game. Besides, it would keep some of the band occupied later once Ted led Tony and Bishop to his main office for a more private chat.

Out here buffet platters with rolled meats and cheeses were punctuated with baskets of cutlery on one sideboard while pies and a tropical fruit salad arrangement took up the far end of the conference table. One of the law partners, a real toad, peered inside and seemed to recognize Tony Silvio.

Tony, ever the obliging showman, smiled and waved through the glass wall.

Ted stopped himself from calling out, "Eat your heart out, bastard." Instead he just winked.

Ted's assistant got Tony Silvio and Bishop settled in with drinks and plates in Ted's quieter office, as Ted turned to his phone to give a quote to someone in the PR department. Tony realized Ted wanted him to listen in on how to share the announcement. Then there was a lot of rustling and a snicker, coming from behind Tony, that made Ted turn around.

The entire entourage of the Tony Silvio Project had made itself at home, legs draped over ornate sofa arms, some crumbs already on the Persian rug, and more than a dozen bodies squeezed into his private office. Tony Silvio was watching with a smile for Ted's reaction.

Ted decided to give him none, other than welcome; this meeting was the top of his to-do list. Ted scanned the room and said warmly, "The Justice for our circuit—"

"Circuit?" It was Tony Silvio himself; the people in front of him turned.

"Each member of SCOTUS," Ted could hear Tony Silvio chuckling—Ted had used the term deliberately and was pleased with the intended effect. "In other words each judge, or justice, is assigned a region, or circuit of the United States. Pennsylvania and New Jersey are part of the third circuit. New York, though, is in the second circuit. Oregon is in the sixth and both Tennessee and Ohio are in the ninth circuit. Those are the states with early landmark birthright legislation." Ted waited in case either man had questions.

Bishop said, "I'm familiar with your past cases opening records in Tennessee after going to the Tennessee State Supreme Court. The same circuit judge who'd be familiar with the Tennessee precedent would be assigned to Ohio, too."

"Check, if legislation like this gets the Governor's signature, we don't even have to go to the judiciary normally. Without both legislative and executive support, you're right, there is an advantage to the administrative judge being the same for both cases, Tennessee and Ohio both being sixth circuit states."

Bishop was back on. He asked a question, "Oregon's prop 58 went before the Supreme Court—it was a public referendum vote without the executive branch backing it up."

Ted answered, "Right, another example of why all our legal energy at the state level was focused on the sixth and ninth circuits on the judicial side. *We needed you activists* to apply pressure at the annual state legislators' and governors' conferences."

"This isn't being left to just one circuit judge, is it?" asked Bishop.

Ted cleared his throat and answered, "If the circuit judge *agrees* that SCOTUS can hear it, *all nine* justices hear it."

Just then Ted's direct line rang.

He apologized to Tony and Bishop and took it.

After a few nods into the phone, Ted caught Tony's eye and said, "This is it. This is the decision!"

There weren't a lot of words exchanged and Ted wasn't betraying anything with his expression. He said good-bye deferentially.

"Well?" Tony asked.

"To Bishop's earlier questions, there are *other* ways an appeal can get resolved. And we just got one of those: ready for this? The Justice who is overseeing our circuit just *denied* the stay!"

Silence. No one in the Club knew if this was good news or bad news.

"They're *lifting* the stay," Ted explained.

"They're *lifting* the stay, they're *denying* the stay," Ted repeated, slightly annoyed that no one was congratulating him..

"Okay," Tony drawled with deliberate casualness, "But when will they hear the case for our kids' rights?"

"They're not. They don't need to. That's the point," Ted said more heatedly than he wanted.

Suddenly Tony clicked in on what he meant but also realized Ted's peevishness was the kiss of death for the energy in the room. Tony took a flier and announced, "Lifting the stay means the Supreme court *agreed to let the law go into effect.* Everyone, WE WON!"

After a silence to let it sink in, some of the adoptees and parents began clapping and calling *thank-yous.*

Ted seemed to want to take Tony Silvio aside and Bishop nudged in, *thankfully*, letting Tony continue, "I know what you're thinking: 'no show', 'no Madison Square Garden'. Think of this stay instead as a million paid downloads of a new song."

Ted rallied, "This win is adding to the weight of precedent that will help activists in other states. The legislators and judges they address will be more likely to make things right because we won and this law *will* go into effect."

For Tony, this wasn't as fun as the Supreme Court showdown he'd been hoping for but it got the same results. He could also see the attorney's glee and he realized Ted was watching him for approval.

Tony Silvio gave it, "However it happened, they're on their feet dancing to our tune. It's got buzz and it's got legs."

Yeah, at least one good thing he'd done this year. Check.

14

Jessica

Maria thought about what she was hoping Tony would do: love a child the way an adoptive father would. Love them, guard them, even without the few extra shared DNA markers. Then she thought about Jessica. She didn't know how to reach out to Jessica. It wasn't even the history of Cyrena and Tony. It was just she didn't know how you bring this kid in. Jessica didn't live under their roof. Tony'd only just met her and she was already grown. Tony might be her biological father but the girl already had both a mother who raised her and a mother who gave birth to her.

There seemed no role for Maria. She hardly ever spoke to her own nieces in Spain. Maybe that needed to change, too, but for now she had an idea. She picked up her phone and scrolled through the menu. Tony didn't know about this, the number she had surreptitiously cribbed from Tony's device. When she found it, she swiped. She listened with her heart pounding to the ring on the other end.

The phone was answered quickly. "Hiya!" came a young voice on the other end.

"Jessica, this is Maria, Tony's wife."

"Wow, Maria, this is kind of a surprise. A nice one I mean. Like, is everything okay?"

Is everything okay? Maria mused to herself. No everything is never okay when your husband is a liar and a cheat and you never know where you really stand or when to trust him. But she also understood that Jessica had a different relationship with the now detoxed Tony. "Everything is fine. Somehow you're family now. I better start acting like it, right? So I just called to say 'hello'."

This was the first time Maria got to speak to the young woman Jessica directly, without Tony. After a half hour or so of chatting Maria asked Jessica how she found Tony.

Jessica explained that he was already in the DNA testing database.

Maria shuddered. That would be true: Tony Silvio had undergone DNA tests to fight off that paternity suit a few years ago. She never asked him out loud how it could be that his adversary had enough circumstantial evidence that Tony's lawyers even needed to resort to a DNA test.

Jessica described for Maria clicking to a webpage that the testing service had set up to display her results.

"On that page, they reported that I had five hundred and thirty-seven potential family members. I went from being a genetic orphan to this. I had no idea where to start."

Maria asked, "You had to sift through all that to find Tony?"

"I was about to," Jessica said, "but then I saw a separate

message that read: 'One Close Family Member.' O.M.G. What? Who?"

This was too fast, thought Maria.

Jessica continued, "I mean, maybe I didn't tell it right, Maria. There were two layers. First, they gave me the option to turn off the 'relative finder' function. That was for relatives as close as second cousins. Once I opted in though, there was a pop-up that explains how this 'new' evidence of a close family relationship can be unexpected and even upsetting. Nice of them to worry about me, right?"

Maria said something about guessing the site wanted to protect her and realized she'd made a mistake when Jessica spat out, "Big Brother knows best, right, Maria?" Then Jessica stopped talking.

Maria felt a flash of embarrassment and anger.

"That's not what I was saying. You should get to know me first. I—." Maria stopped herself. "Jessica, you're right. It's like they're trying to micro-manage you. I grew up under Franco, a dictatorship, in Spain. Old habits of thought die hard. That *was* a little creepy."

Jessica seemed satisfied and continued, "I clicked it, but another warning pops up. It asks me to click 'Yes' or 'Cancel' to confirm whether I *really* want to know who it is.

Maria was eager to smooth things over and repeated, "That was really weird of them."

"Right? Then I have to read more text and mark another checkbox before they'll load the page. Hang on, I'll read it to you. I took a screen shot."

Maria waited while it sounded like Jessica was searching on her device. "Here it is: *You may learn information about your-*

self that you do not anticipate. Such information may provoke strong emotion.'"

Maria wondered, with a rueful smile, why marriages never came with warnings like that. If only the priest told them before their wedding, "*You may learn information about yourself and your partner that you do not anticipate. Such information may provoke strong emotion.*"

Jessica was still telling her story, "...My palms were getting sweaty but I clicked 'proceed' anyway. Then I saw it: **Male, Father, 50% shared, 23 segments**."

Maria felt like crossing herself.

"That's amazing. It was a big change for us, too, Jessica."

Jessica seemed not to notice her words. She said, "There should have been, you know, ringing and flashing confetti like an online game I just won—*50.0% shared, 23 segments!* But it's better than a game. It's real, it's true. It means a lot more."

Maria agreed. She told Jessica that, "It does mean a lot more." She also told Jessica about the anguish of the old paternity suit, all of it.

Jessica really listened. She was hearing a side of her birth-father, Tony Silvio the husband, that she had never thought about before.

Maria hesitated for the words and then was able to say them from the heart, "It was worth it because it reunited Tony and you. You are my family now, Jessica. I think this was meant to be."

There was a long pregnant pause on the other end of the line.

"Thanks, Maria. I don't know what to say. This means a lot, a real lot."

Maria felt a tug just below the surface of thoughts. She struggled to put a name to it and couldn't. She *knew* something around the idea of a paternity test and wished it would rise clearly to the light of day.

15

Bruises

Maria waited next to her carry-on at this quieter boarding gate while small brown birds flitted between potted fig trees her last afternoon in Madrid. She scanned the other passengers, briefly contemplated a woman with salt and pepper hair, black deck shoes with white soles, and a black and white striped crewneck hanging loosely from broad shoulders. A plumped, *femme* Marcel Marceau. Maria looked away to the row of windows. Airfield lights came on and the last rays of sun slicked the fin of their plane wheeling slowly toward this terminal.

Once on board, Maria looked down from the plane window at the baggage handlers and took in their purple and yellow uniforms, headphones like bulging eyes on an insect. She buckled herself in, waiting for one of Madrid's famous sunset skybleeds.

Rapidly falling twilight let the earth darken with the contours of a bruise, blue-black on the tarmac, rising to indigo above the city skyline, finally yellow along the edges of the sky, a wound in the act of healing. She sighed back into her seat for the flight home.

Tony wasn't able to meet her himself at the airport, his message said, but he had a car waiting for her.

When she slipped into his arms that night, she was affectionate but not passionate. Tony raised himself on one elbow and looked down at her. God, she was beautiful. Her pretty face framed in tousled hair. "Maria, what's going on?"

"What do you mean?"

"You know," Tony jiggled her thigh, which usually made her laugh or purr. Instead, she looked up at him patiently.

He sighed and took his hand off her leg. "We've been apart three weeks and there's no locomotion here."

"It must be jet lag."

"You took a nap."

"Tony, there were some years when you came back from touring and we might as well have been brother and sister. You know what I mean."

"Are you saying—?" He knew what she was saying. Damn this. He knew exactly what she meant: what's good for the gander is good for the goose. *She'd stepped out on him in Spain.* She wasn't doing much to hide it. If he had the calendar app handy, he could mark off the exact days she was *incommunicado*.

Was he supposed to thank her for her honesty?

He could kick her out. He was Tony Silvio and he could have a new bedmate by the weekend. He realized she was watching him and it must look to her like he was just staring out to space. He thought for an instant of smacking her like in the movies but there was no way he could see striking that pretty face that was *his*, should have been *his alone*. He knew every inch of her. Loved every inch of her. Deep in his core at a cellular level.

He found himself pressing his lips into hers, pressing himself onto her and she didn't turn him away. She slid her warm hands down his back. When he lifted his chin for air he thought he heard her mumble, "I'm sorry."

Tears shone in her eyes and he reached to turn off the lamp to make them go away. Damn this. He didn't know what to do.

She had always been the faithful one. He counted on her familiarity; he counted on her always being true. Damn this. *He should get angry.* No woman does this to Tony Silvio.

After, he rolled off her onto his back and closed his eyes in the dark. She didn't give him space, instead her arms and lips and tongue worked their way down his chest and her breathing quickened again. He shifted his legs a little and stroked her hair with his hand. He loved this hair, these shoulders, this Maria.

They fell asleep holding hands.

The next morning Tony woke with her nestled in his arms. He didn't like it but he had just relaxed into the idea that they'd get past this.

Then she broke the rest of the news, "...but I was already pregnant when I got on the plane. I'm sure the baby is ours."

He literally saw his rage. White rage. *This was no effing heavenly white light.*

"Tony?" Maria asked, suddenly frozen there in bed. He sat up slowly in a way that chilled her to the bone. This was not him.

He looked at her with hatred. Or hurt. She reached for him but he brushed her hand away.

He fumbled through the junk on the nightstand for his device and hit speed dial. He could barely cough out the words, "Where you at?"

Maria rose on one elbow to watch.

"I'm coming over. You good with that?" he asked hoarsely.

His ears were ringing. He felt like he would suffocate if he didn't get out of here. He might kill her.

He reached down for his pants still crumpled on the floor from the night before and pulled them up as he headed to the hall. As he stumbled down the stairs he heard Maria calling after him. Later he would have no memory of how he got to Rio.

* * *

After Tony stormed out, Maria's mind drifted back to her last day in Spain.

She was in her hotel room and had laid a gold threaded silk shirt she had purchased—an import from Milan— next to the carefully wrapped walking stick. She and her sister found the stick at a woodworker's shop outside Bilbao in the north. The woodworker called it "the staff of Joseph". Its head spumed white roses imitating the staffs of Joseph in the Flemish paintings she saw at the museums in Madrid. The difference was these were carved and then the wood was pickled white at the buds, darker along the staff.

Maria zipped the suitcase closed. There was an hour left before the car came to take her out to the airport.

The room phone rang. It was Elias.

They exchanged only a few words. If she had fallen in love with him the lightness of his farewell would have stung. He was not obligated, she decided, to come see her off and so she was content with just this. *Better to be happy.*

Besides it eliminated one of the arrays of choices she was weighing in this last hour. Now she knew that Elias' and her tryst was complete, that is to say, finished.

She knew also that she loved Tony still.

Maria thought of the stick she had left resting on the bathroom sink enamel. A plastic stick.

With a clear pink line finally. She was pregnant.

During the year Jessica was conceived, Tony gave Maria chlamydia. Somewhere in the span of years since then he gave her HPV. It was nothing short of a miracle to see this pink line.

She knew it before she took the test, she may have even known she had conceived before she arrived in Spain but she couldn't be sure. She did know she would carry this child. How many years had she waited to feel this fullness, to see this little pink line? But she could not say with certainty who the father was, Tony or Elias.

Then a thought drifted up. Maria remembered that Jessica and Tony both took DNA tests, Jessica to find her birth-family, Tony, earlier, in that paternity battle. Tony's results would still be on-line. She knew his user key and password. He used the same ones for everything, of course.

Somehow, if she also tested the baby's DNA and they came up a match, the affair could be forgotten. She would have to administer this test to the baby in secret in case they were *not* a match.

If the child turned out not to be Tony's, to be Elias', it was clear that she and Elias would not parent together.

She looked over at the suitcase thinking of the staff of Joseph and the golden shirt, suddenly feeling another pang of guilt. Would Tony welcome her child with another man? *As Joseph welcomed the Holy Infant born by Mother Maria?* Just as she was learning to welcome Jessica?

Then just as quickly she felt no guilt. She had forgiven Tony. Many times. Tony Silvio, ladies' man, would he forgive her one dalliance if she told him she carried the child of an affair? Jessica was conceived when they were already dating. Maria hoped he would forgive her, too, but that was out of her hands. That was a decision that rested in *his* hands and *his* heart.

* * *

She would carry the child. That was one decision made.

In Madrid, she told herself there was another choice for her: to not test paternity at all. She could keep herself as innocent of knowledge as she might keep Tony.

1. She *would* carry this child.

2. She would *not* confess to Tony the affair.

3. She would *not* test her child's paternity.

She hadn't been able to stay with the decision to hide the affair even twenty-four hours. *Sitting here now in their empty home, she understood why she changed her mind. Lying just wasn't who she was.* As she traced spirals over her baby, she made another decision. *Not testing would ultimately be unfair to the child. And the child's descendants. There.*

1. She would carry this child.

2. She confessed to Tony the affair.

3. She would test her child's paternity after they were born.

If Tony insisted that she surrender the child, as Jessica had been surrendered, she would face a different decision. But that was unlikely, she mused while lying across the hotel bed in Madrid, because Tony trusted her and would therefore assume the child was theirs.

Now, alone in the empty house she saw that she had read Tony wrong. Rio, she hoped, just meant Newark and sitting down to work it through with his sponsor.

* * *

Two weeks later, Tony and Maria found themselves hurling another set of volleys only an hour before a press conference. *Damn this before he had to go on.* He slammed out the door.

Maria was sitting on the throw rug in their room and felt the wall she was leaning against shake when Tony slammed the door. She breathed and then looked down at her still flat tummy and started tracing concentric circles around her navel. She pushed the fights out of her mind and thought about quickening, what the midwife described as "feeling like champagne bubbles popping inside you." She couldn't wait to feel that and it was supposed to start in a few weeks.

An hour later Tony Silvio stepped onto the stage to see a small stadium of faces, television cams and all manner of devices pointing up at him. They twinkled like a white electric Christmas. Even after that miserable bombshell from Maria,

Tony Silvio *still* loved *this* whole scene. For the first few moments he tried to tell himself that it'll be about the concert and book tours, The Birth-Fathers' Club court case of which he was the star, or his long sobriety and paying it forward. Tony Silvio was ready.

He pointed to a dude with glittering hair for the first question.

"Will you be raising your wife's lovechild the way others raised Jessica?"

Wife's lovechild. Others raised Jessica. Tony almost reeled off the stage to attack the questioner who was smiling smugly in the second row.

How the hell had they got hold of this already? He had barely learned of the pregnancy himself. Now it would be out there for the whole world to read about. *This could have all sorts of ramifications across the Tony Silvio Project.* He tried to tell himself it was *only* about the Tony Silvio Project, the business, but the rage that was choking him told him it was more personal. *Lovechild.* They were all up in his business, his private business. How the hell did they get hold of this?

It could *not* have been Bishop or Fred, he was certain of that. They all had kept far too many secrets for him to think that they would leak this one on him. *Lovechild.* Could be one of Maria's friends, or someone at her doctor. Still, he had to marvel at these obnoxious on-the-spot wordsmiths and how they managed to dig up even the smallest, most deeply buried scrap of dirt. He certainly had something eloquent himself to say about the visibility of *where* they could *stick* that question.

But just before Tony could lean into the mike to deliver the choice words, Bishop the Glove threw an arm over his shoulder, the rhythm guitarist grabbed his arm, and Bishop leaned into the mike.

"Tony and Maria have been together for over twenty years. They've made the Tony Silvio Project a family. All of us are rooting for them. If you know them at all, you know that whatever decision they make—it will be mutual and in the best interests of the band and the fans that make up our family."

The press bank popped with lights, roared with questions and the stage door opened to more paparazzi than usual.

Bishop hustled Tony and the band outside, pushed Tony's head down into the waiting van, made him lie down across the back seat to keep him out of view. Then Bishop quickly climbed in and called up front, "Jameer, floor it!"

The scene didn't get any better in the penthouse. When they got back, Maria was in one of the side bathrooms bent over the porcelain throne heaving. Bishop, always the fixer, beat Tony by a half step and offered, "I'll take care of this."

Tony tried to push past him anyway. Then he heard Maria sob and he broke free of Bishop. Tony's and Maria's eyes met for just a minute, hers teary but even, before she bent over the john again. This was his wife, he pulled loose strands of her hair back just in time. From the toilet bowl he heard a muffled, "*thank you.*"

Then, he faltered, wasn't sure what he wanted. That could have been the moment for Tony to say, "I love you," or "It's gonna be okay." Instead, he gave the nape of her neck a peck and turned to Bishop and said, "Get her to bed. I'm going to shower." As he headed for the master suite he had another idea and headed down to the garage.

* * *

Tony Silvio hummed as he headed two hours out to an old EDC site to soak in the silence. Then stayed for four days. As a tribute he also didn't take a shower.

At least he didn't use and he didn't drink. He brought his Stratocaster and its clumsy power ensemble with visions of practicing old solos that echoed off the walls of this canyon space. He also brought along an acoustic for variety and practicality, in case the power apparatus glitched on him. It happens.

The guitar was a Conde Hermanos that he and Maria found in a basement shop on a visit to Spain. They found it on a rainy day a few *calles* from the Teatro Real in Madrid. He walked in and got wowed by their legacy. Leonard Cohen, just before he died, revealed he'd been playing a Conde for his whole career and thanked them. They hadn't realized the skinny kid who came into the shop forty years earlier would be a star. There were photos and vinyl from other stars who played their guitars, from Bob Dylan, to underground flamenco and tango musicians.

When Tony picked up one with a cypress soundboard, one of the *hermanos* looked at him with new respect. He came out from behind a workbench and walked them through the details of the fretting. The guy didn't recognize Tony Silvio and so with Maria interpreting between Tony's English and Conde's Spanish they had a serene conversation about the luthier's art. Back then Tony didn't get to have much of that between touring and the crazy that was life as The Tony Silvio Project. The instrument had the bright, percussive sound that Tony liked.

He'd always thought of acoustic as the shy cousin of electric but this guitar was different. It cut, whined and wailed.

Now, happy to be sitting alone on his first morning at this well-known venue Tony pulled out the Conde. You could smell the wood and he paused to appreciate the handiwork of the rosette. He showed off for himself, pulling out a riff that had him running chords up and down the frets while he used an old pick. He lost himself and lost track of time until the pick broke. Damn, he loved this. He reached for some ice water and checked his phone. No service, which was fine, and he saw he'd been playing straight up for two hours totally into it.

He thought of Maria and this time it didn't hurt at first. When the pain came back he poured it into a melancholy Argentinian tango he'd learned in that basement years ago. He and the shopkeeper had sat facing each other on the workbenches, playing off each other until he got the knack and they were able to meld into a dark duet with that signature pulse that came from the Argentine goldmines. At the end of it, the *hermano* pointed to the curved body of the guitar that Tony held and said through Maria, "This is Spanish cypress, it grows straight up. All over the Mediterranean it's found in cemeteries. They say it brings the souls resting there straight up to heaven."

Tony had never been able to sample tango into his songs. He tried once not long after he and Maria got back from that Spain trip, weaving some of the notes into a slow, heavy stadium Metal piece. It wasn't right back then.

He looked at the still rising sun and thought he'd give it another try. He decided to experiment with another key and tightened on a clamp. He took another swig of H_2O and fingered through the chords breaking them down slowly. The cold air was starting to warm on his neck as he played. He was hearing the notes and their connections new. He already knew this would go somewhere.

16

〰️

The Backstories World Tour

Life goes on. The outdoor concert season started, and they had a full schedule. The Tony Silvio Project announced The Backstories World Tour playing twenty-five cities across Europe, East Asia, and the Americas. The four days at the abandoned arena kick-started Tony's creative juices and he had two new songs to show for it. There wasn't much time to learn and rehearse them. The unfamiliar tango beat was a challenge but the guys added a few new licks that made each tune their own. Especially good timing because this year welcomed the first rave venue for the Tony Silvio Project, and the tango percussion tracks added a new feel.

The rave was honoring the late DJ Avicii who, it was said, planned to sample some of their classics. Now the fans would get to hear the originals overdubbed by a DJ the Tony Silvio Project was bringing out. Just when that was set, Tony's publisher threw Bishop a curveball but he was able to get their last seven concerts rescheduled, basically the month of September, to clear the schedule for Tony's book tour too. As it was, they were playing almost every three days straight from May through August.

Then the Glove sent Jessica the schedule so she could pick the locations she wanted to attend. When Jess got back to her newfound father, she asked for tickets for two more friends and they added her to the list for Belo Horizonte, Brazil, Quito, Ecuador and the 3Arena in Dublin, all relatively small arenas so Papa Silvio would have something resembling free time back stage.

* * *

Warm up bands were playing as the skyline turned indigo and licorice pink. Tony stayed backstage after their afternoon mike test but the roadies came tumbling in with reports on all the kinds of people filling the stadium there at Red Rocks.

Pete, their sound engineer noted it all gruffly with, "Amen, Jesus. I hate the smaller music fests where all you get are goths with Vapes."

With this one, size meant variety. All kinds of people were converging on the natural amphitheater in the foothills of the Colorado Rockies. Pete added appreciatively, "They say Red Rocks has been known for its acoustics since the days of fiddle bands." His last statement was punctuated off in the distance by a newly arrived group that was whooping as they stared over the edge of the cliffs down at the stage. Tony squinted up at them and they waved excitedly.

The mood was getting better for Tony and he surveyed the setup behind them. They had rehearsed together well, some of the backup band had been with The Tony Silvio Project for years, and they'd gotten this out of the way: said what needed to be said for the fallen artist Avicii but acknowledged their own bond in recovery.

Bishop was nearby, talking into a phone, not yet pestering anyone about time. He was pacing around under a three-fourths cube of 26 flood lights that would come on during the stadium anthem "*Crystal Lights, Diamond Nights*". There'd been a glitch when they played the castle at Castle Donington in the UK. It was the fifth stop and Bishop the Glove was following up to make sure it didn't happen again on their touring season.

Tony heard one of the canvas banners flap which immediately drew Bishop's attention too. The wind was picking up but Tony decided that this was a good thing when he saw it spirit the last few white clouds westward. It would be a clear, starry night for the fans. Just then a grip walked up to them carrying a small cooler and offered them choices in bright colors. Tony declined and in a minute another artist who Tony almost didn't recognize gestured toward him holding a bottle of European mineral water. The performer came over and Tony accepted his offering but sniffed it first to make sure.

The guy was a Canadian DJ who was known for wearing a mask early in his career. They sat down on some boxes and the DJ lifted his own bottle of beer in tribute.

"I've always wanted to meet you, man. You introduced your style, which gave me the courage to introduce mine, you are the badass of style."

Tony burst out laughing but the guy was achingly sincere. They clinked bottles.

This was a long way from the Tony Silvio Project's acoustic songs. Turns out those were the best ones arranged for this thumping electronic beat. The Canadian and he talked about that a little. Then the guy's girlfriend came up to them and he draped an arm around her as she showed Tony her new tat. It read, "Everything is beautiful. Let the music carry us together."

It suddenly struck Tony as poignant. That was the rave lifestyle at its heart. He was getting used to it. Not too far from the early days of rock'n'roll, he mused. He felt his phone vibrate and took the call when he saw it was Jessica.

There was a lot of giggling on her end, happiness not nervousness, he couldn't make out much of what she said because it kept breaking up.... "Love you, Dad...like you're the Tony Bennett of electronica these days."

He laughed, made a few jokes back at her, sad and relieved to hang up as the background noise of the crowd grew louder. Damn reception. He finished the mineral water and nodded at the couple.

"Hey, Pete," Tony called as he jumped off the box.

Pete squatted into a wrestler's post and Tony dove at him. Immediately Bishop was hovering over them like a chaperone. Tony and Pete stepped apart as Bishop brushed red dust off the sleeve of Tony's shirt. Tony finally felt loose and he turned to Bishop and asked, "After the show, can you get me a line to Rio?"

Bishop let surprise cross his face before nodding obediently. Tony knew this was no small feat and would cut into Bishop's enjoyment of the next couple of hours. That's why Bishop got paid the big bucks, Tony reasoned.

Bishop was about to begin working his phone when he hesitated and turned back uncertainly to Tony, "You haven't been in touch with Maria at all this tour...?"

"Nope," answered Tony and didn't give Bishop any hint more.

Then their cute, young makeup artist appeared up the red dusty trail from behind Bishop and she was carrying the rest of Tony's wardrobe: belt chains, scarves, earrings. She gestured toward the makeup booth and Tony followed her inside, thank God, it was air-conditioned with a generator.

They joked and flirted as she dabbed on layers of warpaint and finished with strokes of eyeliner, her lips and breasts just breathing distance. Once she was done and she passed him the hand mirror, she asked what he was doing after the show.

Tony surprised himself and answered, "Ain't Misbehavin'. Going to sleep." He gave her a twinkle and nothing more before adding, "Showtime, darlin'."

* * *

Six hours later, Bishop stuck his head in the door and pointed at his cell phone. Fred was on the line back in Newark. Tony popped it up to his left ear.

"Hey, can you hear me okay? This is an encrypted line Bishop set up for us."

"I can hear you fine. But I'm worried. You've never needed this before. Are you okay?"

"All the PCP made me paranoid."

"Are you being serious?"

"Nah, they really *are* out to get me, I'm not paranoid."

"I promised I'd always be point blank with you and you promised to be point blank with me: are you using again?"

"No. Serious. I'm clean and sober. Safe and sane."

"Good. What's with the secure voice line?"

"They already caught one of the paparazzi trying to plant a bug backstage. They brought in extra security for the venue but it's *Get Smart* when it comes to cybersecurity: I either talk into my shoe or use whatever this is Bishop arranged. It's been crazy since all the rumors about Maria being pregnant." His mind was racing like it always did after a gig this big. He hoped Fred could help him center down.

Fred sounded cheerful now, relaxed, "...I saw it on the news. You looked great, but...why are you calling me?"

Tony couldn't bring himself to the topic yet. "The sound was amazing at Red Rocks, clear and sexysonic and the crowd was tight with us. Every last one was tight with us. Damn. God-speed to 'em. Onstage it was so effing cool. Fred, there were these guys who'd hiked right up these red cliffs to look down on the whole scene, the crowd, the stage, the band. It was so effing cool," and Tony paused for effect, "but here I am calling you two hours later. From the tour bus. In a hotel parking lot in Denver."

"You did the right thing. You called instead of losing your sobriety or your abstinence, right?"

"Damn straight. But this effing, situation with Maria. Did I tell you she's not on the tour this time? Eff her. I'm glad she's not. She wants to take it easy, she says. Eff her. She's just using me, she doesn't give a damn, she just wants— she just wants—"

"Woah, woah, and where have *resentments* gotten you in the past?"

"But she went out and fucked another—"

"You're calling. I'm asking: where have resentments gotten you in the past?"

"Wasted.   High.   OkaaaaayI'mmmmCaaaaalming-Dowwwwn."

"Good. Tony, I'm here. You did the right thing calling. What's got you 'restless, irritable, or discontent' as the ol' AA Big Book says?"

Neither man spoke for a solid minute. Tony sat down on a plush, upholstered loveseat and kicked a cable running along the wall of the tour bus. Pete's girlfriend, who got silly but not in an annoying way, had led some of the girls in plastering the inside with sticky notes to make a point that was funny at the time. They had labelled every pillow, every mug, and every awards night photo up on the wall of the band's doublewide until Bishop kicked everybody out.

The party would continue inside the block of suites they had booked in the hotel on the other side of the parking lot. Tony was alone finally. Now he sat picking off the neon paper squares into a crooked pile on a table in front of him as he gathered his thoughts. He turned Fred's question over in his mind.

"What's got me 'restless, irritable and discontented'? When this gets confirmed, if it gets confirmed that the kid's not mine, I'll look like a *fool*. I'll *have to* ditch her then."

"Why would you have to ditch her? If it's about ridicule, looks to me like you survived that press conference just fine and you didn't even know it was coming. You looked good on your feet. Hell, *you've* embarrassed yourself far worse in the past. So, if it turns out the kid isn't yours, then what?"

"I should kick her out." He hated when he had to spell it out for Fred.

"'Should'? Says who? And we know how good *you* are at playing by the rules, so it's not very authentic for you to be talking about 'shoulds'. As your sponsor, here's the *only* question that matters: *what would help and not hurt your recovery? What would strengthen your serenity?*"

Fred had a way of reframing things, Tony had to admit.

"Tony, I'm not saying that what you're feeling isn't justified. Or that this isn't 99% the other person's fault, but you know the big three: resentment, fear, harm. What's the resentment here?—*don't just go off on me*—find the words for it. Then what's the fear behind this for you? Then, you know the drill, what's the harm *you* caused?"

"Nah, no. Just give me a moment here." If he kicked Maria out, he'd be kicking out his best friend. An abortion wasn't an option—she was serious and would kick *him* out before *that* happened. He got what was underneath it all.

"Fred?"

"Okay."

"I hate that she was with another guy. I just hate the thought of anyone else touching her. But I know what you're going to say: dig deeper. Got that. So it's not a fear that she'll leave because it's clear she came back to me. It could hurt sales—"

"Hang on. This is deeper than sales. I agree she's already made her mind up by coming back to you. And by telling you the truth about the affair. But what I think just happened is that she made you realize another fear. Fear of losing her, you *love* her that much."

"Yeah. No. I don't know. Maybe."

"You know the next question: what's the antidote to fear?" Tony felt Fred's voice pulling him along.

"Faith. She came back, see how it goes. Gotta have faith," said Tony. "She did come back, yeah. Resentment? That she was steppin' out and I can't call her on it. I did plenty of that, too. So I got nothin' to say here."

"Now you're burying it, Tony. Remember that line, 'I can't afford to resent anyone or anything because it will lead to another slip?'"

"Straight up 12 Steps. Yep, I got it but..."

"You've got to flip the script or the resentment will boomerang on you. *You* decide your spin, *you* decide your history, what can you replace the resentment with?"

Tony paused until he heard himself say slowly, "My best friend is finally going to have the child she's been hoping years for."

"Tony, that's *it*!"

"But I can't forgive that *sonofabitch* who slept with her. I owe him nothing, no forgiveness."

"Fine. Who said anything about forgiveness? Try acceptance. Accept that they slept together. Accept that you don't get to claim the high ground on that one, my friend. Accept that the woman you love who is your best friend is finally going to have a dream come true. Accept that you won't know for nine months whether it's *not* your child. Save yourself nine months of grief, it won't change anything. But if you don't accept this situation, it may cost you your sobriety and your marriage."

There was a sense of "rightness" about what his sponsor was saying. It moved him what Fred was saying.

"My life is never like anyone else's," Tony half-whined although there was some pride as well behind it.

Fred didn't miss a beat. "Oh, what's that called? Having to be better than or less than? *If* it turns out this isn't your biological child you will become one of the *millions* of men now and throughout history who have parented a child they didn't father. Maybe you need to write a thank-you note—to Jessica's dad."

"Pow."

"Write a thank-you note, with true humility and gratitude, to Jessica's dad. If you have trouble, call me. Or better yet, get down on your effin' knees and pray on it!"

Tony swallowed. His thoughts were calming down enough to feel howling pain. He wanted a stadium to break into a riot.

Cracking chairs over cracking heads.

Tony swallowed again, came back to the here and now, and thanked Fred. Hung up. Reminded himself of the 12 Step slogans, *Feelings aren't facts* and *This too shall pass.*

Then Tony Silvio actually reached for a pad of paper in the top drawer and scratched out a letter to Jessica's adoptive father. When he was done, he rolled into one of the upholstered benches, exhausted but surprisingly calm and satisfied.

As he drifted off, Tony thought about how much had changed—in him and for him—in the many months since his phone rang and he heard Jessica tell him he had better sit down. He knew he was still the crazy, self-centered compulsive person he had always been—prone to running from trouble or lying his way out of situations, feeling sorry for himself even when he created the problems, thinking about himself and his pleasure first.

And yet he also saw that he was changing, slowly, for sure, but changing nonetheless. He thought back to how impassioned he had been when he talked to Dan about being a father; he thought about Jessica's adoptive dad loving her and raising her, and his own feelings of love for her once he got over the shock of her existence.

Yes, Maria was important to him, more important than he ever wanted to admit in the past, and she deserved a chance to be a mother. It was something they had been denied, and he realized that with the chance before them he owed it to her to be the best father to this child ever—whomever the genetic father turned out to be.

With that, Tony fell into a deep and easy sleep.

17

Last Waltz

Tony smiled appreciatively, "This stuff's legit. Sorry about the circumstances though."

Ted smiled expansively. His two least favorite colleagues just walked by and clearly recognized the celebrity musician through the glass of his office suite. If Ted Landtsman had to go out on *their* terms at least he would leave them wondering if they'd regret who they'd messed with.

"Corporate culture is more and more like the arts in that it's a gig. It's just a gig. You get what that's like," offered Ted.

Tony nodded and spread some Almogrote cheese that had been flown over from La Gomera in the Canary Islands that same week.

Ted had known for some time that the natives were restless, meaning the other partners at the firm. They were managing him out. He'd seen it coming but he wanted to go out in style. Ted wanted to have Tony Silvio up one last time on a day when all the *sonsabitches* senior partners would be in the building.

He'd heard that Tony liked tapas with fine *jamón ibérico de*

Bellota. When he learned that Tony Silvio's wife was Spanish Ted decided to go a little more upscale *and expense it.* He ordered up some Spanish-Japanese fusion dishes from the new place off Park Avenue. They didn't disappoint. The delivery was beautifully packaged, they dined on cloth napkins, silverware and five-glaze porcelain.

Tony seemed comfortable splitting a platter that mixed Kobe beef cuts with samplings of regional *chuleton*. Then they finished the main course by sharing a fresh kettle of steaming *paella* fused with Japanese seafood *nabemono* with an interesting zest of ginger.

"Tony, I've got a request that I wouldn't normally make to someone like you. I'm one of the biggest attorneys in the city."

"You're shorter than my keyboardist." That was too easy. Tony quickly leaned forward and poured Ted more sparkling water to soften the zing.

"Good one, Tony. Good one," Ted shot back obligatorily.

"No, I got it. You're a prominent guy."

"Right. I understand personal branding. Not getting caught in the weeds or letting your brand suffer overexposure so I wouldn't normally make this request, Tony, but there is a group that formed from the birth-fathers we identified while we were looking for birth-fathers to testify. It's called the Birth-Fathers' Club," said Ted quickly.

Tony considered his host patiently, "I know it. Remember Clay is a neighbor of mine? Maria knows his wife and he's the one who brought that kid Dan backstage."

Ted nodded and looked a little embarrassed before continuing his explanation, "Clarence Dennen has been the driving force—the front man if you will—of the Birth-Fathers Club but supported by my PR staff."

Tony eyed the Harvard pinkie ring on Ted's hand, the high thread-count shirt, the tailored suit, the Italian leather shoes and for the first time saw them as the armor of a small but scared man, certainly an intelligent man who meant well. *Ted didn't get where he was by always being a good man but, Tony mused, we've all got a past, and now Ted seems to be trying to do the right thing with his life—taking on the court case for free and all.* It made the ostentation lovable.

Tony smiled genuinely at his host, "Aw, cut the preamble. What is it you want?"

"The Birth-Fathers' Club is having a one-time farewell dinner. It's part breaking down the band, part a way to give everyone a night out. There are adult adoptees and donor-conceived people who want to find their original families, but still can't. It's also a thank-you. To search angels, volunteer genealogists, who help with search and reunions. To activists for their work through all these years of court cases and legislative lobbying, including birth-parents. To the adoptive parents who stepped outside their comfort zone to advocate for ethical adoption practices. They deserve it. And *you*," Ted leaned forward and pointed affectionately at Tony, "*you* lend the whole thing cachet. Some even came on board to volunteer after they heard you took time out from your schedule to testify."

"You got a venue yet?"

"Clay is paying so I was going to let him pick. If you're there I can justify having my firm pick up the tab for security."

"I'll do you better," Tony exclaimed, "Have it at Tony Silvio's. Best Nebraska-bred bison and ostrich with a ginger ale infused marinade. Salad bar. Sugar plum pies are in season right now. My chef uses them with just a hint of black cherries in a tart wrapped with a cinnamon-layered crust—you've never tasted anything like it, man. Same for the shrimp and avocado marsala. I am not kidding you. But it would be a one-evening engagement. I'll have them reschedule any reservations and close the house just for the Birth-Fathers' Club."

* * *

The next day Maria went to the drugstore. Her eyes widened when she saw shrink wrapped pregnancy test kits that promised to tell how far along a pregnancy was:

Less than one week.

Two to three weeks.

Three weeks.

Over three weeks.

Less than one week and Elias was the father.

Two to three weeks and she wouldn't be absolutely sure who the father was unless she tested the baby after the birth. Three weeks and it was Tony's but close enough that he would never believe her.

The last option, three weeks *plus* would show she was pregnant before she left Tony for Spain. She pulled a box down off the shelf and added it to her basket. She couldn't wait to get home.

Maria followed the directions, then recapped the stick, and prayed for two minutes.

The first test kit didn't work.

Luckily, she bought a three pack. In anticipation of the second test she not only had her usual morning *café con azucar*, she drank chamomile tea and a tall glass of orange juice. She was ready to try stick number two before she went to the gym.

* * *

Maria came home from the gym to find Tony sitting by the phone. He was throwing back what looked like a twenty-four-ounce water bottle. He looked at her with a twinkle and said, "I got some news and figured I needed a drink before I told you."

Her heart skipped a beat. This wasn't funny. The bottle must be filled with clear vodka.

She wanted to cry, to hit him. She made a grab for the plastic bottle and instead he tripped her and scooped her into his lap.

She smelled his breath. No liquor. He was laughing. "Angel, I'm keeping my sobriety. I said I needed a drink, I just made it a water."

He laughed again and told her about the legal stay, and the party, "at Tony Silvio's to celebrate the decision by the Supreme Court of the United States, baby!"

Finally, Maria relaxed.

One day at a time, she reminded herself.

Then as she felt a quiet joy seeping in, she turned to her husband, "There's more good news, Tony. This baby is yours. Ours."

She explained the test and then started for the powder room. He followed her. There it was, digital letters still reading "Pregnant. 3 + weeks."

Tony Silvio whooped and sang, "I was there for the conception, baby! That was me." Tony felt he kind of knew the baby was his all along. "That was me! Come 'ere Mama Silvio!"

And his wife did just that. Long into the night they celebrated the little Maria & Tony Silvio Project.

Reading Club Discussion Questions

1. Should Jessica have contacted Tony? Did she have a right?

2. Both Bishop the Glove and Fred guide Tony. How are they similar and how do their roles differ?

3. Tony is compared to St. Joseph and to Jessica's adoptive father despite obvious differences in lifestyle. In what ways are the three men similar?

4. Was Tony too concerned with Maria's feelings about Jessica? Was he not concerned enough?

5. Why does Maria stay with Tony? Would you?

6. How did 12 Steps in this book match what you already knew about the addiction recovery program? How did it differ or what did you learn?

7. How did Fred and Tony use the 12 Steps for something other than recovery from addiction?

8. In what ways, big and small, does Tony find redemption?

9. Do donor-conceived people have a right to contact a DNA parent?

10. If you're feeling imaginative, or playful, which is your favorite Tony Silvio song: "*Big Hair Love*", "*Crystal Lights, Diamond Nights*", "*Shoot the Alarm*", or "*Wedding Vow Hearts*"?

About the Author

Michele Kriegman is a storyteller by nature but she was missing her own backstory well into adulthood. Finding her birth-father helped complete it. She is the second child her birth-father placed for adoption before he entered the foster care field professionally. She worked many years in Japanese and U.S. journalism, including Nippon TV's morning show and ABC News. More recent journalism has been for cybersecurity publications, all under her adoptive name.

Reclaiming her birth-name, Suzanne Gilbert, she began curating virtual bookshelves of reunion fiction and non-fiction while writing the novel, *Tapioca Fire*, that is the prequel to *The Birth-Fathers' Club*.

She speaks on topics as diverse as "#OwnVoices: How to Write Your Spiritual Memoir", "Waiting, Creating, and Finding Family: Past, Present, and Fiction", and "Transnational Adoption, Human Trafficking, and Triggers". She also wrote and performed "The Baby Shower", produced by Cyndi Freeman, *The Moth*. Michele/Suzanne {she/her/hers} lives in a multi-species household.

More at:
https://www.reunionlandpress.com
https://twitter.com/ReunionLand
https://www.facebook.com/ReunionLandPress